THE MAN IN THE HOUSE

Emmy Ellis

M. A. Comley

PROLOGUE

Flowers in the garden, one, two, three.
A rose, a tulip, a forget-me-not for thee.
Red nails, pink nails, or a purple hue.
Taken away to keep… A part of you.

He stood and watched, the sound of the nearby sea whooshing.

They were there, the police, inside her house on the cliff top.

Smaltern. A shitty little town.

He thought about what he'd done and clutched the sewing kit to his chest. The threads had closed up what needed to be closed. They'd stopped her talking. Stopped her doing…*that*.

The officer at the door had been staring down at his feet for a while, mind probably elsewhere,

1

wishing he was in bed instead of on a doorstep in the middle of a cold winter's night.

It had gone well.

Sad and angry that it had come to this, to what he'd had to do, he walked across the open-plan front gardens, keeping out of sight behind the hedges that separated the pavement from the lawns. At the end of the cul-de-sac, he turned the corner and strode away, slipping his kit into the pocket of his black trench coat. He bent his head, his fedora pulled low to shield his face.

Callie had told him once not to behave like he was the only one to make all the decisions. But he'd had the last laugh with her.

He'd become the man in the house.

CHAPTER ONE

Helena stared down at the bloodstain on the beige-patterned carpet.

"DI Stratton!"

She turned, holding back a sigh, telling herself not to be a bitch to him. That wasn't who she was—or who she used to be anyway. She was allowing her past to define her, and she needed to chill the hell out and stop poking at her partner.

DS Andy Mald stood there in all his late-fifties glory, glaring at her from behind his thick-lens glasses with their black frames. Sounded like someone had pissed on his parade.

That'd be me again. Be nice now. It's not his fault you have issues.

His brown, grey-speckled fringe flopped over his forehead, and one of his shirt buttons was undone in the middle, probably in his rush to get down here. Hairs poked through, coming out to say hello.

"Yes, Andy?" She gave the blood her attention again. The stain wasn't right, as though someone had poured it there instead of it seeping from the body.

"You didn't call me out." Andy came to stand beside her. Too close.

She took a step away, breathing through her mouth. "Thought you'd rather be in bed." This wasn't what she needed, him getting up her arse because he hadn't been included. Who the hell would want to be called out to a murder scene in the middle of the night if they didn't have to?

Him, obviously. Mr Know-It-All.

Prat.

Stop it…

"Well, you thought wrong, didn't you," Andy snapped. "We're meant to be partners. Half the time, you're off on your own, like some lone vigilante. It doesn't work that way. You have to make sure I'm with you, and you *know* that. Look at what happened when you did that before. You said it wouldn't happen again, yet here we are…"

Same rant, different day.

Bloody cracked record.

She tuned him out, otherwise she'd bite his head off, and that was becoming a regular occurrence lately.

While he blethered on in the background, she studied the body. Female. Brunette. Twenties. Naked. A pretty thing, makeup perfect, although the blue on her eyelids was a bit nineteen-eighties. Maybe that look was coming back into fashion. Helena wouldn't know. She hadn't owned a makeup bag in years, and even then, she'd only worn mascara and a bit of foundation.

She stared at the face of the woman on the floor.

Her mouth.

Oh God…

"…and what about that time you kept information to yourself and didn't tell the team? You can't keep doing *that* either."

All right, so Andy was getting on her tits now. Much as she wanted to rein her temper in, she couldn't.

"Oh, be quiet, will you?" she said. "I'm trying to think."

"Rude, that's what you are." He folded his arms across his chest.

"Yeah, well, you're not telling me anything I don't already know, mate."

He was right. She *was* rude. And bitter. And angry. She'd tried to like him, but honestly…

How his wife had stuck around for as long as she had before she'd left him was beyond Helena. He was a nonstop complaint merchant.

Remind you of anyone?

Oh no, she didn't need Marshall in her head. They'd been seeing each other for six months but had split up recently—his temper wasn't something she could tolerate. Its appearance had become as constant as Andy nipping at her nerves, day in, day out.

She was better off single so she could—

"What's there to think about?" Andy asked.

She closed her eyes briefly. "What part of 'be quiet' didn't you understand?"

"Christ, you're a mardy bitch."

I'm mardy because I'm sodding well stuck with you.

"I ought to tell on you," he said.

She laughed. It was either that or clock him one. "Really? *How* old are you?"

Helena stepped round to the other side of the body. Anything not to have him so near. He stank, and it reminded her of the past and what she was trying to heal from. Smelling him every day was becoming too much. She'd snap soon, and then where would she be? Hauled into Chief Yarworth's office, having her arse chewed.

"She lives here?" he asked, pointing at the corpse.

"Yes. Sole tenant. Callie Walker. Single. Works in Waitrose."

"SOCO been and gone?"

"Um, no. You should know that. Didn't your little desk sergeant buddy tell you?"

"No."

So he wasn't denying it that she slipped him info then. Andy fancied Sergeant Louise Baker, all six feet, blonde hair, and blue eyes of her. He bordered on being a ruddy pervert, always flirting and finding ways to brush past her. Helena cringed on Louise's behalf every time he did it. If he went too far, she'd have to call him on it. Women being objectified pressed her buttons.

And you know why that is.

Car doors slamming gave her a reprieve. She walked from the living room, into the hallway, and stood at the open front door, ignoring the uniformed officer standing off to the side on the grass. SOCO had arrived, and after putting on their whites out on the plastic-sheet-covered path, she stepped aside so they could file past her. Zach Forde, the ME, pulled up to the kerb next, and she went to the pavement to give him the basics.

"Hi," she said, her heart doing that annoying thing it did whenever she saw him. Pattering too fast, bringing on butterflies. Christ, she needed to pack it in, fancying him.

"Hello, you," he said. "What have we got?"

"A woman. There's blood, but even I can tell it isn't from her—unless she's got a wound I can't see. There's not a speck of it on her, just a pool on the carpet next to the body. She has a scarf round her neck—you know, the chiffon sort, got some bird or other all over it, might be a starling—so I can't see if she's been strangled." Why had she mentioned the birds, for God's sake? Babbling, that was what she'd been doing, like some young girl.

If she wanted him to like her, that mascara and foundation needed to make an appearance. And she couldn't let him like her. Not really. There was Marshall who'd get arsey, and then there was—

Fuck it.

"I'll have a look in a minute," Zach said. "But we can have a natter here until the photos have been taken, if you like?"

She rubbed her arms. "It's a bit nippy…"

He held his hand out to his car.

She nodded.

They got inside, and it was still warm from when he'd driven here. She stared at the cul-de-sac, the road and pavement a weird mix of grey and amber from the streetlight standing behind a blackthorn tree with its birthday suit on. At three or so in the morning, it was quiet. A few neighbours nosed from behind partially open bedroom curtains, splashes of light behind them, their figures silhouettes.

"How's things?" Zach asked.

She cringed. Why had she told him she'd split with Marshall?

You know why.

"Um, still not good." She bit her lip.

"Why don't you just report him for bothering you then?"

"It's not that easy."

"Of course it is. It all went south, so you ended it. Simple, really. The fact he's still hanging about…"

She didn't turn, didn't need to see his face to know he was frowning. Jesus, she'd got herself into a right old mess, hadn't she? She couldn't even remember *why* she'd liked Marshall in the first place. He was a bit of a knob, if she were honest. Bold, brash, look at me I'm God's gift. Maybe that had been the attraction in the beginning. A man like him wanting her after what she'd been through… Had that been the appeal? For her to feel desired, loved, not used just for sex?

"He'll go into one," she said. "Like I told you, he's got a temper. I don't *do* men with tempers, you know that. It brings back memories."

"I understand that side of it, but how many people do you tell to leave men like him? How

9

many people do you encourage to get restraining orders?"

"I know, but they don't always work, do they." She sighed. "Some men don't feel the law applies to them, and Marshall fits that bill. But I'll do it—I'll have a proper word with him." *At some point.*

"If you ask me, talking to him now isn't even quick enough. Leave it too long, and he could do something to you." He paused. "I'm here, you know."

She wasn't sure how to take that. "In what way?"

"In every way."

"I see." Her heart rate escalated.

"Do you?"

"I think so."

"Well, you know now, so…" He cleared his throat.

"Yes, I know." She threaded a gloved hand through her hair. "We're a right old pair, aren't we?"

"We are. I thought you'd have realised how I felt when I split with Kirsty."

"I didn't like to presume." *Or hope.*

A rap on the passenger window jolted her, spoiling the moment, and she snapped her head round to look at who was there.

Andy.

She should have guessed he wouldn't keep out of her air space for long.

"Don't let him bug you," Zach said.

"I can't help it. He's like vinegar on a burn."

Helena flicked her hand at Andy so he'd step back, then she got out and stood in front of him on the path. "What?" There she went, being a cow to him again. She hated herself for it.

"SOCO have found something."

"Right." She stared at him. "Are you going to tell me what it is, or do I have to guess?"

"Guess." He smiled like a kid.

"You're such a prat, man."

Pissed off with his games and him in general—*and* her wreck of a life—she walked back up the path and into the house, changing her booties for a fresh pair, her gloves, too. In the living room, she approached a SOCO who knelt beside the sofa. "What have you got, Tom?"

He jerked his head for her to come closer.

She crouched and peered down into the shadows at the carpet beneath a square end table. "What the hell?"

Pink gardening gloves with roses on them had been laid on the floor, red fake nails pressed to the ends. Four lines of what appeared to be blood-soaked salt created the semblance of two arms. She kicked herself for not having spotted it herself when she'd first arrived.

"Okay…" She held off a shudder.

"Bit weird, isn't it?" Tom said.

"And the rest." She stood and nodded at the gloves. "No clue what that's meant to mean."

She stepped back ready to walk away and trod on something.

"My toe, Stratton," Andy said.

Helena closed her eyes and gritted her teeth. She faced him and smiled tightly. "Sorry, but if you weren't right up my jacksy, I wouldn't have stepped on you, would I?"

"Blimey, what the hell's got your goat? You need Kalms or something, woman," he said, shaking his head.

No amount of over-the-counter stress relief would help her in this moment. They weren't suited as a partnership. They rubbed each other up the wrong way. She needed a new right-hand man or she'd end up in the clink for stringing him up by his balls.

"And you need Right Guard or something," she whispered. There. She'd said it. Got it out in the open.

"Oi, there's no need for that," he said, bristling.

"Oh, there is, believe me. Buy it. Use it. Or I'm going to have to tell on *you*."

His cheeks flared red. "That's a bit below the belt. I can take most shit from you, but not that."

"No, no, please don't get the wrong end of the stick. I'm not being mean." *For once.* "It's something you need to sort. Seriously. People have noticed. They've mentioned it. Do you want to be called in for a chat with the chief? That's where it's going to end up if you don't do something about your...problem."

He rubbed his forehead. "Honestly?"

"Yes."

She walked away, guilt pinching her gut. She couldn't bear the smell of him. It brought back memories. Reminded her of *him* and—

Don't.

Zach came in then, suited up, and she'd never been more pleased to see him. The overhead light brightened his blond hair, and he smiled at her in that way he shouldn't.

Not while we're at work.

"Over there," she said, pointing to the gardening gloves, "is one weird-arse present left for us."

He peered over. "Oh. Lovely." Then he glanced at the body. "I hope those nails on the gloves aren't hers."

A shiver prickled up her spine. "Her hands are underneath her so..."

"Am I good to start work?" Zach asked Tom.

"Yes, she's been photographed."

"Thanks."

He walked over to the body. Helena followed and, if her sense of smell was spot on, so did Andy. She blushed at what she'd said to him. She should have delivered it in a better way — and in private. Tom had undoubtedly heard her. Maybe she'd done them all a favour by opening her mouth, but still, she should have had more tact. Him poking at her meant she'd retaliated in turn. She should know better. Should have pulled him aside. The fact he was an annoying git shouldn't have influenced her to speak out.

Christ.

Turning to Andy, she said quietly, "Listen, about what I said…"

"I'm going to go home," he said. "I'm not needed here."

"Right." *Fucking hell…*

He left the living room, and she almost chased after him. To say what, though? The damage was done. She consoled herself with the fact that everyone on the team had complained to her about him.

I shouldn't have been such a bitch.

"Bollocks," she muttered, staring at the ceiling.

"Helena?"

She blew out a breath and joined Zach. The victim's hands were out by her sides now, the ends destroyed from having the nails ripped off. She had to be a fresh one — no rigor mortis —

14

unless she'd been killed way before now and it had already come and gone.

"Um, that's…not nice," she said, then called over to Tom, "They *are* fake nails on the gloves, aren't they?"

"Seems like it."

So unless Callie Walker's nails were in the house somewhere, her killer had taken them.

Zach took Callie's scarf off.

"Oh." Helena winced. "So she *was* strangled."

The slim line of livid purple bruising on her neck appeared to have been made by a rope or something of that nature. Her tongue wasn't sticking out, though, which didn't mean anything because… Helena didn't want to look at Walker's mouth again. The first time she'd seen it had been gut-churning.

Lips sewn together with thick, red cotton was enough to put anyone off taking a second glance.

She imagined the killer stuffing the tongue back inside so he could use the needle on her lips. And wished she hadn't. Her skin went clammy, and she gritted her teeth to divert her attention away from her thoughts.

"Yes, strangulation," Zach said. "That would be my first impression, based on petechiae on her cheeks and the burst blood vessels in her eyes, but it could be something else entirely. PMs come in handy for that sort of thing."

She laughed a bit. "Sarcastic sod."

Zach leant over Walker and checked inside her ears. "No blood there." He lifted her head to look at the back. "No trauma. I'd say you're right—that blood isn't from a wound."

"We'll soon find out if it belongs to her," she said.

"Yep. And if it doesn't…"

"Hmm." She'd sift through the possibilities, but really, she couldn't face it. Not yet. "Any signs of sexual assault?" She folded her lips over her teeth and pressed down hard, waiting for his answer, praying he didn't say yes. She closed her eyes so she wasn't tempted to watch him check between Walker's legs.

"Oh," Zach said. "Bloody Nora."

"Do I want to see this?" she asked.

"Probably not."

Helena opened her eyes anyway.

Callie Walker had been sewn up down *there*, too.

CHAPTER TWO

It had been one hell of a morning, and it was only half eight. Suzie bit the inside of her cheek so she wouldn't explode on the kids. They were messing her about, running around the living room. Loons, the pair of them.

"Pack it in," she said, "and for the love of God, get your bloody shoes on."

They did—eventually—and within ten minutes, they were all out of the door and on the way to school. Ben and Toby shot off ahead, leaving her panting to catch up. She'd had a right old time of it trying to lose weight after they'd been born, and what with it being so much easier to sling a pizza in the oven after work, the calories lived on her backside. She hated it but didn't have the money to buy all that fresh food Jamie Oliver went on about.

"Or the time to cook it," she muttered, staggering on.

The school appeared around the corner, and she legged it as best she could over the playground and into the kids' cloakroom. Her lads, twins, fucked about throwing plimsolls all over the place, and one whacked a girl on the head. So mass hysteria didn't erupt, Suzie apologised to the mother and grabbed her boys by their arms.

"Sit down, change your shoes, and stop being so naughty," she said through gritted teeth, giving them The Glare and The Voice, the ones that told them she really, seriously, had had enough.

They obeyed.

With them packed off into the classroom for the poor teacher to deal with, Suzie bustled off to pop their school dinner money envelope in the deposit box beside the sliding window belonging to the receptionist. It was cardboard and wrapped in artwork created by a couple of nursery children. God, it seemed ages ago now since Ben and Toby had been that small. Where had the past seven years gone?

Back outside, she zipped her coat up. The wind had a nasty bite and tossed her long hair about. If she hadn't been so distracted this morning, she'd have put it in a bun, but everything about the day so far had just about set her on the road to Hell.

Again.

She turned the corner into her street, readying herself to tackle a bit of cleaning for half an hour before she had to get down to Waitrose for her shift. Ten until two, she did, which helped bump up Robbie's wages. The days of them squandering their cash prior to getting married were long gone, and the money Mum had left her in the will had been spent fixing the broken tiles on the roof, and hadn't that cost a packet. An arm and a leg, Dad would have said.

Why had they bought this house again?

You know why. You had to get away.

She unlocked the creaking wooden door and stepped inside, sighing at the bomb site. You wouldn't think she'd tidied up after the boys had gone to bed last night. Why did she bother? It was a pointless task, a never-ending recurrence. The lads' pyjamas were strewn on the living room carpet, and one of them had eaten his breakfast on the floor in front of the TV—not allowed; he must have done it while she'd been in the shower, the scamp. He'd left the bowl there. A dirty sock sat inside it, soaking up the leftover milk.

Suzie had to fight not to cry.

"Come on, you silly cow, just get on with it."

In the zone, she cleaned up, made the beds, and scrubbed the loo and sink — why was there always toothpaste left around the plughole? Every. Single. Day.

Christ, she needed a holiday.

Without the kids.

The doorbell rang — just what she bloody needed — so she went back downstairs to answer it, out of breath and narked that a neighbour might be after something. A toilet roll, a bit of juice, Calpol for a grizzly kid, or any number of sodding things in her almost bare food cupboard. Why was she the street shop?

She flung the door back and snapped, "What!"

A woman and a man stood there.

Oh. She hadn't expected that. She blushed and wished she could shut the door and open it with a nicer attitude. Or better yet, wake up all over again and approach the day with a sunnier outlook.

The woman's short brown hair was in a trendy pixie cut, and she was pretty as anything, maybe around thirty-eight or so. The man was older, pushing sixty Suzie'd bet, and a strong scent of aftershave came off him.

That might cause Suzie a problem if they hung around for long.

"Suzie Naul?" the woman asked.

"Yes…" Who were they, and how did they know her name? Shit, she hoped they weren't from the council tax. She hadn't paid it for about four months now, and they'd already had a nasty letter. Or three. Suzie hadn't had the time to give them a ring to sort some kind of payment plan—there weren't enough minutes in the day—and if she were honest, she was scared to speak to them about it. Then again, she didn't really have to. Robbie was due a bonus on Friday, so they could pay the lot off then.

"I'm DI Helena Stratton." She held up ID. "And this DS Andy Mald. Can we come in?"

What, they sent the police out for not paying a bill now? Wasn't it court first, then the bailiffs? Or had she got that mixed up and it was the other way round? Had they got a court letter and Robbie hadn't told her?

Suzie's heart fluttered then plunged into deep pounding. She'd be sick in a minute if she didn't calm herself. "I can have the money to them by next week," she managed to get out, rubbing her chest. It hurt. She'd think of it as her asthma rather than an oncoming panic attack.

"I'm not here about any money, Mrs Naul," Stratton said. "Please, we really do need to come in."

"Oh. Christ, has something happened to the kids or Robbie?"

21

"No," the copper said, stepping into the house and forcing Suzie to move back.

Mald came in, too, and the hallway was crowded, enough for Suzie to contemplate screaming. She didn't like being in close quarters with people she didn't know, and that bloke's aftershave was getting to her chest.

She rushed off into the kitchen, grabbed her inhaler, and opened the back door, gulping in air. Sucking Ventolin into her lungs, she held her breath for the required ten seconds, then exhaled. She repeated the process, her chest finally relaxing a bit. Her face burned, and she flapped her hand in front of it.

"Are you all right?" Stratton asked, coming in and standing beside Suzie.

"Yes," she said. "His aftershave… Asthma."

"You should have had a whiff of him before he put that on," Stratton whispered and winked.

More at ease now, Suzie brushed past her and moved to the kettle. "Can I get you some tea? And will you be long, only I've got to leave for work in ten minutes."

"You might want to ring in and say you can't make it," Stratton said. "And sit down. I'll make the tea. You look like you could do with taking a moment." She pointed at the small dining table with four chairs, one of them pulled out already where the good child of the day had eaten his breakfast there.

Suzie did as she was told, staring at the remains of chocolate boulders and brown milk in a bowl. Why would she need to stay home? What the hell was going on?

Mald came in, and Stratton beckoned him over to the open door.

"Stand here," she said. "Your aftershave's a tad on the strong side, and Mrs Naul has asthma and can't breathe."

"And *I* can't win," he mumbled.

Suzie frowned. What was that all about? "Listen, you're worrying me. If it isn't the kids, or Robbie, or that bloody council tax, what is it?"

Stratton patted Suzie on the shoulder, then went over to switch the kettle on. It wouldn't take long to boil, seeing as Suzie had used it recently. The copper took three mugs off the tree on the worktop and put teabags and a sugar in two and four in the third. Suzie was overweight, but pissing hell, did Stratton just assume she had a sweet tooth?

"When was the last time you saw your sister?" Stratton asked, leaning against a cupboard, comfortable as you like.

Suzie frowned. "Which one? There's two of them."

Stratton glanced at Mald, and he took a notebook out.

Had her sisters got themselves into trouble? She couldn't imagine that, unless they'd slept

23

with someone's boyfriend or husband and had been found out. They were a bit too free with their favours in Suzie's opinion. They wouldn't ever knowingly encroach on another woman's bloke, but saying that…they were damn good at keeping secrets, so who was Suzie to say whether they kept ones she didn't know about?

"What are their names?" Stratton asked and poured water into the cups.

"Callie and Emma…"

"Both Walker, yes?" she asked, squashing a teabag on the inside of a cup.

"Yes. Look, what's one of them done?" Suzie glanced at the clock. "And I'm going to be late for work. I'm meant to be leaving in a minute or so and I've still got to get my uniform on."

Stratton poured milk then brought the heavily sugared cup over and placed it on the table. "Have a drink. Just 'be' for a second, all right?"

"I haven't got that luxury," Suzie all but snapped. This was getting on her bloody nerves. Why couldn't the woman just come out with it?

Stratton collected the other cups and handed one to Mald, who took it with a grunt and placed it on the windowsill beside the back door. Suzie would normally have a go about that, saying the heat would mark the recently glossed wood, but something about the uncomfortable silence meant she kept her mouth shut.

Stratton sat opposite her. "Has Callie got any enemies?"

So it was Callie they were interested in. Suzie had the mad urge to laugh. Callie with an enemy was like the queen without a corgi. It just wouldn't happen. Well, apart from *him*.

"No," she said. "Not that I know of." Another check of the clock sent Suzie's heartrate scattering. "Why don't you just visit her? She can answer any questions. I'll give you her phone number and address, and you can get on with it." She took a sip of tea and winced at the sweetness.

"Okay, I'll make the questions quick," Stratton said. "Then I'll get to the point, all right?"

Suzie nodded.

"Does she have a boyfriend?"

"Not at the moment."

"Does she like gardening?"

"What?" This was getting well annoying now. "No! She hates it since —" Shit, it had nearly popped out. She'd have to make something up now. "Since she helped Mum cut roses and a thorn pricked her finger." God, that sounded so *stupid*.

"So she wouldn't have owned gardening gloves as a rule then?"

"No. Our brother sorts her garden because…" *Fuckfuckfuck*. "He mows the grass, does a bit of weeding."

"I see. And his name is?"

"Jacob. Walker."

"Right. Does Callie wear false nails?"

"No."

"Does she use nail polish?"

"*No*." Suzie's guts rolled over, and she stared at *her* bare nails. No colour for her or her sisters. Definitely not. Just thinking about polish sent her back to a time she'd rather forget.

"So no red nails then?"

Could you faint sitting down? You could, couldn't you? Suzie's balance seemed shot away, and her chest constricted. She puffed on her inhaler again.

"Are you okay?" Mald asked, coming closer.

"Step back," Stratton said. "I've already said why…"

Mald retreated with a *hmmph*.

"It's okay," Suzie managed, but it wasn't. It really wasn't. Flashes of memory flickered in her mind—red nails, pink nails, purple nails…*him*.

Oh God, oh God, oh God…

"Is there anyone we can call to come and sit with you?" Stratton asked. "I'm concerned you're going to have an attack."

"I haven't got *time* for an attack. Please, I need to go to work. I don't understand your questions."

"Can Emma come round for a bit?"

Anger boiled then, and Suzie slapped her hand on the table. Tea sloshed out of her cup. "I can't afford not to go to work. Can you leave now, please, if you're not going to say what you're here for? I have to get on. Really." She stood and stared at each of them in turn, her cheeks hot.

The police weren't budging.

Suzie flopped back down, all the fight fizzling out of her. She never had been able to stand up against people who gave off vibes of authority, of being stronger than her. If anyone stared at her for too long, she backed down immediately. "What? What's happened?"

"You're the oldest of your siblings and therefore their next of kin, yes? No other family about?" Stratton asked.

Suzie blinked. Why was she needing to know that? She opened her mouth to ask.

The doorbell ringing put paid to that.

"I'll go," Stratton said.

"It'll be my brother," Suzie said. "He drops me off at work sometimes."

Stratton left the room, and murmured voices filtered through from the hallway. Stratton and

Jacob appeared, and tears itched Suzie's eyes at the sight of him.

"Sit down, please," Stratton said, eyeing Jacob as though he was a creature from another planet.

Jacob frowned and raised his eyebrows at Suzie. She shrugged back, and he settled beside her, reaching out to take her hand. She didn't want his comfort but couldn't exactly say so when they had company. If he touched her, she might break down. Today had been a shitshow and a half already.

Stratton took a deep breath, looking as though she wanted to be anywhere but here. "I'm sorry to have to inform you both that your sister, Callie, was found dead in the early hours of this morning."

Suzie's lungs refused to work. She managed to grab her inhaler, tried to take a breath, but blacked out.

CHAPTER THREE

A lilac forget-me-not was outside Suzie's door
when she went upstairs to bed. Her tummy
tightened, and she wanted to go downstairs and tell
Mum, but he'd said she couldn't. If she told, Dad
would die, then Mum, then Callie, then Emma, and
finally, herself.

She got into bed, quietly so as not to wake her
sisters.

In the middle of the night, he crept in as he always
did, and touched her in places he shouldn't touch. She
closed her eyes and waited it out until he went away
again, the sound of the back door opening barely a
whisper. He'd be back, but until then, she'd sleep and
pray to God, who never listened, even though He was
supposed to.

Tomorrow, she'd have to put purple nail polish on so he could see it and know she was still keeping her promise.

That she wasn't going to tell.

CHAPTER FOUR

"That's not something I thought we'd be doing," Andy grumbled. "Waiting for a bloody ambulance. It's taken up a good bit of our morning. It's almost lunchtime, and my sandwiches are back at the nick. At this rate, I'll be eating them for my tea. That Jacob was a weird-looking chap, don't you think? Recessed eyes. They always give me the willies."

Helena didn't feel in the mood to talk about someone with a weight problem so she ignored Andy's griping and drove on, turning towards the coast, where Emma Walker lived in a cottage on the Smaltern cliffs. With house-to-house enquiries going on in Callie Walker's street, Helena and her team needed to do the other side of investigating. "Ring Olivia for me, will you, and see how she's getting on with the social media accounts of the Walker family. Then ask Phil if anything's turned up in his background searches."

"They always ring if they find something, though," Andy said.

"You can never just take an order, can you. Is it because I'm a woman or what? I've always wondered." She was sure that was his problem—he kept failing the inspector exam, and her coming in to take over from his previous male partner a few years ago had clearly boiled his piss.

Andy snorted. "Don't pull that card. It's because what I just said is true. They *always* ring—and you *always* badger them before they're ready to give us info. Do you know how irritating it is to have someone breathing down your neck when you're trying to work?"

No, she didn't. Not these days anyway. Their chief, Damien Yarworth, was a lazy bastard who let her get on with things. He didn't ask for updates, knowing Helena had it all in hand. She was glad. Running to him every five minutes would get on her wick.

She had a think about what Andy had said, and he had her there. She *did* prod and poke when she didn't need to.

"Fair point," she said.

"What, you're not going to deny it, biting my head off while you're at it?"

"No. Can't be arsed."

They continued in silence for a while, a couple of minutes that seemed like twenty, what with the body odour issue hanging around between them—except now it was excessive aftershave. Should she say something about that, too? It had been over the top for Suzie Naul, so it stood to reason it'd be too much for other people.

Bugger it.

"I'm not picking, I swear to God I'm not, so don't go all high and mighty on me, but can you tone the new scent down a bit?" she asked, cracking her window an inch.

He sighed. "Christ Almighty. Do you want me to beg for a treat and all? I thought it'd be better than the *other* smell." He sighed again, this time not his usual, affronted sort.

"It is. But it's just that you don't need to use so much. If you're spraying deodorant, you shouldn't even need aftershave to mask anything." Helena turned down one of the quaint cliff top streets with their cookie-cutter cottages that featured on many of the postcards in the local tourist shops.

"I let myself go, didn't I," Andy blurted.

"Excuse me?" It was the only thing she could think of to say. In all the years she'd been working with him, she'd never heard him admit he was in the wrong, let alone that he might be struggling with life—assuming that was the issue.

He rubbed his chin. "When Sarah left. You know…"

"I see. You didn't go downhill when she first went, though. It's only been the last year or so."

"I wanted her to come back, so I…"

Helena got it. He'd kept on top of things, thinking she'd return home. When she hadn't… "It happens," she said, feeling sorry for him. "People split up." She thought of Marshall and how she'd told him to take a hike. He'd got angry, torn her a new arsehole, and still bothered her from time to time, but in the end, he'd be out of her life when he realised she meant what she'd said. She'd move on—but she wouldn't forget to spray Dove.

"I stopped showering, cleaning the house, all that sort of thing." Andy spoke as if she wasn't there, almost to himself, a revelation he was just now seeing. "You should have said I stank sooner."

"I thought it'd pass—the phase or whatever it is. When it didn't…" Should she open up a bit herself? "Listen, you know the Uthway case?"

"I'll never forget it."

Nor would Helena, but for completely different reasons to Andy. "Your smell brings back memories of…"

"Oh. Shit."

"Yeah."

"I'm so fucking sorry."

Helena swerved into a space between two cars outside Emma Walker's. "No sympathy, please."

"I didn't realise."

"No, you were caught up in your own problems, and that's as it should be."

"But that's been a year of you putting up with it. The reminders…"

"Yep, but let's forget it. So long as you wash your armpits and whatnot, we're good. We've got this poor cow to speak to now, so let's get cracking."

Andy rested a hand on her shoulder, and Helena turned to look at him.

"I'm not an arsehole deep down, Stratton," he said.

"I wouldn't know. We've been partners for years, and you've always come off as a bit of a wanker—sorry, but that's the truth. Show your other side. No one likes a dick."

"Let it all out, why don't you."

"I would, but it'd take all day, maybe even into tomorrow, and we have to be getting back to work."

He stared at her as though he wanted to say more. About Uthway.

"Don't," she said. "It'll be fine. I'll get over it." *No, I won't.*

She got out of the car and waited for him to do the same. He was massaging his temples in circular motions, so she left him to it—if he needed a minute or two to get himself together, she'd give it.

She stared between two houses on the other side of the street. The dark-blue sea stretched beyond, a grey line separating it from a light-grey sky dotted with black-bottomed cumulus. A storm was well on the way. The wind would pick up soon, chugging the scent of brine and kelp with it. Gulls squawked overhead, spreading the news for everyone to stay inside before thunder rolled and lightning staggered, its reflection looking back at it from the sea.

Andy got out of the car, and they walked up Emma's path.

"All right?" she asked him.

"Not really. Maybe we should have a drink after work. Clear the air. I've been thinking of all the times I was a knob to you."

"That'd be nice," she said. "But don't expect me to be sorry for thinking you're a knob all this time."

He laughed quietly, and Helena knocked on the door.

"Put it all away for now," she said. "We have a job to do."

Emma Walker opened the door and stared at them. It was obvious she hadn't been told a thing—unless she was good at holding her feelings in. Her eyes weren't red-rimmed, her skin was rosy but not blotchy, and she had a casual pose, not the hunched one of someone who'd been given devastating news.

"Yes?" she said, tilting her head so her brown ponytail swung.

"Hello. I'm DI Helena Stratton, and this is DS Andy Mald. We need to talk to you about something. Can we come in?"

They showed their ID.

Emma frowned, her blue eyes narrowing. "What about?"

"Your sisters." It wasn't a lie. One was in hospital, and so was the other, although she wasn't on a ward. The poor cow was probably under Zach's knife at the minute.

"Suzie and Callie? What's happened? Has something gone off at work?"

Earlier this morning, Helena had done the background on the sisters—Suzie worked at Waitrose, same as Callie. "Um, no." She raised her eyebrows and gestured at the door. "Shall we?"

"Of course." Emma stepped back and pressed her bum to the wall, a full body shake going on. "Are they okay?"

She seemed overly panicked, more so than anyone Helena had met on the job before. Emma bit her bottom lip and clenched her hands.

"Let's go and sit somewhere, shall we?" Helena said.

Andy closed the door, and Emma led them into a living room. Helena blinked. Everything, including the walls, ceiling, and carpet, was black.

"Oh, wow," Helena said.

"I don't do colour," Emma said.

It sounded cryptic, an undertone running through it. Emma shuddered and rubbed her arms, sitting on the leather sofa. Her torso appeared to hover in all that blackness, her dark leggings disappearing, only her white, long-sleeved T-shirt, her head, hands, and feet distinguishing her from the surroundings. She had a dragon tattoo on the top of one foot. Black.

Helena stood by the door, and Andy sat on an armchair, notebook in hand.

"I take it you haven't spoken to Suzie or Jacob this morning?" Helena asked.

"No. I haven't texted Suzie since yesterday, and Jacob contacted me last week. Wednesday, I think." She bounced one leg.

"What about Callie? When did you last speak to her?"

"Um, last night."

Oh, now we're getting somewhere.

"Was that by text, Messenger, on the phone, or did you see her?"

"She gave me a ring around eight o'clock."

"And what did you talk about?"

"She thought…" Emma blew out a noisy breath. "She thought someone was in her back garden."

"I see. What happened then?"

"I stayed on the phone with her while she went next door to ask the bloke there to go and have a look."

"And did he?"

"Yes. No one was there. Callie's…she's jumpy. She thinks… Well, she just sees things or thinks things that aren't there. She's always saying there's a man in the house. She's…not right."

"In what way? A mental issue?"

"Oh no! No, nothing like that. I just mean…she's a bit nervous. Any little noise, she thinks someone's breaking in. She rings me about that sort of thing a lot."

"Do you know why she'd think that way?"

Emma hesitated a bit too long. "No." That was a firm answer.

A lie?

"Was there a problem with someone? Had she had an altercation with somebody for her to think they might be in her garden or want to break in?"

Again with the hesitation, plus a quick glance at a photo on the wall. "No."

Helena studied the picture. All four siblings together, Jacob standing at the back between Suzie and Emma, his arms around their shoulders, Callie in front, kneeling. A studio portrait, and all of them looked uncomfortable. That wasn't surprising, seeing as those types of settings didn't exactly inspire relaxation or ease in front of the camera.

"Do you have a friend who can come and sit with you for a while, as we have some upsetting news."

Emma's mouth went slack, and she stared between Helena and Andy as if waiting for one of them to deliver the wicked, verbal blow. "I...no, I don't have many friends, and they'll all be at work now."

Emma worked at The Villager's Inn, a pub a mile or so down the coast, so Helena assumed she maybe did the evening shifts.

"Okay." Helena gave her a sympathetic smile. "I'm afraid that after us visiting Suzie to give her the news, she had an asthma attack and had to be taken to hospital."

Emma gasped and went to say something, but Helena carried on.

"Jacob is with her, so you don't have to worry there, and we were assured she'll be all right. She just needs to be on a nebuliser for an hour or so. Do you drive? We can take you if you need a lift."

"What?" Emma shot up and hugged herself. "What news was it?"

"Take a seat again, Emma," Helena said.

Emma flopped down, arms still across her belly. "Oh God, it's Callie, isn't it?" She rocked and gazed vacantly out of the window. "I can't do this again, not after Mum and Dad."

Checks earlier had shown Mr and Mrs Walker to be deceased, the father when the children had been small, the mother recently, around five months ago.

"I'm afraid so," Helena said gently. "She was—"

"Murdered," Emma said, her eyes filling. She remained staring through the window, although she probably wasn't registering anything outside.

That was a strong statement… Does she know something?

"I have to ask… Are you aware of anyone who would have wanted to do this to Callie?"

Emma's face crumpled, and she sobbed. Helena waited for five minutes while the woman cried it out and Andy went off to make Emma a cup of sweet tea. He returned and placed the black cup in Emma's hands, and she sniffed and whispered a thank you.

"I should have driven over there," Emma said. "Last night. But she's forever saying someone's trying to get her, so I thought it was just the same old rubbish." Her lip wobbled. "And now I feel bad for saying that. It wasn't rubbish. Someone must have been there."

Helena supposed it was an easy assumption that Callie had been killed in her home, considering the evening phone call and what Callie had told Emma. "Yes, someone must have been there. Now, I'm going to ask you a couple of questions, because something was left in her house, and we really do need to find out what it means. Suzie doesn't feel they belong to Cassie. I'd like to know what you think, all right?"

Emma nodded and looked up at Helena. "Okay."

"Would Cassie have owned a pair of gardening gloves with red roses on them?"

Emma's sharp intake of breath was loud — she hadn't been quick enough to hide her reaction. "No. She hated gardening. J…Jacob does it for her." Emma shivered.

"What about red nails. Would she have had those?"

"Absolutely *not!*" Emma almost shouted, then seemed to check herself. "No. No way. She hates nail varnish."

"Any reason why?"

Emma clamped her mouth shut.

Something bloody weird was going on here. Why would anyone be so averse to having their nails painted red?

"Emma?" Helena prodded, anxious to get some answers.

"She..." Emma closed her eyes for a moment. "She just doesn't like it, that's all."

"Did anything happen in relation to red nail varnish?"

"I don't want to talk about it." Emma plonked the cup on the floor beside her feet. "I need to go and see Suzie." She sighed, and it came out shaky from the aftereffects of her earlier sobs. "How...how did she die?"

"Early indication, strangulation."

Emma wailed. "Did he...did he do anything else?"

He? Is that a guess it's a man?

"I'm not sure the details are something you need to hear at the moment," Helena said. "This has all been a bit of a shock, and you don't need the extras."

"I do." Emma glared at her, either anger or determination stiffening her spine. "Believe me, I do."

"If you insist. I'm incredibly sorry to say she had her mouth and vagina sewn up."

"Oh… Oh no. Fucking hell…" Emma rammed her knuckles between her teeth, and she shook all over. She lowered her hand. "I should have said something."

"What about?"

Emma blinked, seemingly confused, then she blushed. "About…about…I don't even know what I mean."

Helena had a feeling she did, but poking Emma about it could wait until tomorrow. Yes, something was definitely off, and Helena was determined to find out what the hell it was.

CHAPTER FIVE

*T*he artificial pink tulip was outside the bedroom
door. Emma swallowed, thinking of how the
forget-me-nots for Suzie had been there only last
night. He usually visited them once a week each,
giving them time in between, so to have him in the
room a second night on the trot meant...

He was getting worse.

Emma's 'session', as he called it, wasn't due for a
few days. She hadn't prepared herself. Hadn't spent
the week so far gearing herself up for it. She shivered,
glancing around the landing as if he skulked in the
shadows, and she peered through the bathroom
doorway in case he was in there, waiting. But he
wouldn't be. He only ever came in when Mum and
Dad were asleep.

Emma went into the bedroom. The lamp was on beside Callie's bed. Both of Emma's sisters were asleep – or so it seemed. Had they seen the tulip, too?

She stared at Callie's bare nails, then at Suzie's purple ones. In the morning, Emma would have pink on hers, and next week, Callie would have red.

Emma looked around. Pink wallpaper, pink bedding, the typical room for girls. She hated it. When she was older, her bedroom would be black and white. Her whole house. She wouldn't have reminders then. At least not indoors. Outside, though, life lived and breathed colour, every shade imaginable, and she'd always recall what he did, would always remember nights like...this.

Him.

She was going to tell Dad, no matter what he'd said.

Come the morning, everything would be all right.

She switched off Callie's lamp.

"Why is there another session so soon?" Callie whispered in the darkness.

Emma jumped, her heart racing. She sat on Callie's bed and reached out to stroke her sister's hair. "I don't know."

"Will it be my turn tomorrow?"

"I hope not." If Emma told Dad, it would all be okay, wouldn't it? There would be no more flowers, no more painting nails.

"We mustn't say anything," Suzie said from her bed in the corner.

Had she read Emma's mind?

"No, we mustn't," Emma said. But she'd tell — she'd just ask Dad not to say how he'd found out.

Emma patted Callie's head then got into her bed, the one in the middle of the row. She stared at the dark ceiling, squinting to make out the dragon shape created from an ancient damp patch where the water tank had leaked in the loft years ago. It was directly above her head, and she stared at it when he came in and...did what he did. It was her anchor. Her way to pretend it was a giant beast in a faraway land where fairies danced in meadows and castles dotted the horizon.

She loved dragons.

CHAPTER SIX

With a small glass of white wine on the table in front of her, Helena leant back on the green fake Chesterfield sofa in the pub. Andy sat on one of the chairs opposite, a pint in hand. Guinness, the top creamy-looking, about an inch thick.

"Why did we choose this job?" she asked, thinking about the day they'd just had.

Andy sighed. "If you mean, did we sign up to chat to all the staff in a supermarket to find out who bumped their colleague off, I don't know. If you mean, did you know your wife would leave you because you're never home, I don't know."

Shit, he was a bundle of laughs, wasn't he?

"It still gets to you after all these years then," she said. "Sarah leaving."

"Of course it bleeding well does. We were with each other from fifteen years old. We'd planned to grow old together and all sorts." Andy took a long pull of his pint. Some of the froth clung to the skin above his upper lip. He wiped it off with his sleeve. "Turned out she decided getting old with someone else was more her style. Maybe he can give her the babies I couldn't, although her having children at our age... A bit dodgy, isn't it?"

Helena didn't want kids, so she'd never thought about what age was best. "I'm sorry that didn't work out for you. But going back to the copper bit; she knew you wanted to be a policeman. Surely she was aware of how much you'd have to work—the odd hours, being called out in the night and all the other bollocks we deal with." Helena took a sip of wine. It tasted bitter. She'd get sweet next time.

The Blue Pigeon was a stone's throw from her house, so she could manage a second glass and not have too much alcohol in her system for work the next day. Andy would have to get a taxi—he could forget about kipping in her spare room. They'd walked from her place to the pub, Andy wittering on about the house-to-house enquiries not yielding any results apart from the next-door neighbour who'd come to check the garden. Andy had also banged on about there being no visible evidence other than the weird gardening gloves and those creepy-as-eff nails. Oh, and the fact that social media had thrown up jack shit, just a few friends in common.

"She was all right until I made detective," Andy said, eyeing the floor between his feet as though it had the answer to everything. Then he looked up. "Shall we have some dinner while we're here?"

Helena nodded and reached for a menu wedged between a Sarson's vinegar bottle and the salt and pepper shakers, a bottle of Heinz tomato sauce standing forlornly to the side. "Could do. We never did have any lunch, did we."

"No, and I'm bloody starving. Got a steak on there, have they?" he asked. "With chips and peas, none of that rabbit food stuff."

Helena ran her finger down the steak section. "Nice sirloin here. They all come with chips and salad. I could always ask them not to put it on the plate, you know." The image of a chicken sizzler platter with onions and peppers caught her attention, so she'd have that and make her own wraps.

She got up and walked to the bar, thinking she'd pay, seeing as Andy was down in the dumps. Placing the order, she waited for the barman to tot it up on the till and thought about Andy's behaviour over the years. Why was he such a douche? And, more importantly, did she want to know? Wouldn't it be better just to ask for a new partner—someone with less baggage? Then again, she carried a few suitcases around herself, so she was a fine one to talk.

Helena returned to the table and plopped back on the sofa. "Right. We're here to talk about our working relationship, not the case. I've bought your grub, by the way. You're welcome."

His eyebrows shot up.

She laughed. "Don't look so surprised. I'm not really a cow deep down—similar to what you said about yourself. So spill the old beans, will you, because elephants in the room are always unwelcome guests."

"You saying I need to lose a bit of weight?" Andy patted his overhanging gut and grinned.

"Fuck me, is it your birthday?" she asked.

"Eh?" He frowned.

"You smiled." She reached for her glass, drank some wine, and eyed him over the rim.

"Very funny, Stratton." He twirled his pint around on the table. "I've just forgotten how to be happy, that's all."

Well, that just went and dumped a load of guilt on her, didn't it.

"Sorry," she said. And she meant it. "Want to talk about it? Let's start with why you're that knob I call you so often—which I shouldn't, and I'm truly sorry I do it."

Andy shrugged. "I don't know, I'm just angry all the time. Sarah's gone, and I don't think she ever laughed like that when she was with me."

"So you've seen her with him then? Her fella?"

"Might have."

Helena gaped. "Please don't tell me you followed them or something equally weird."

Andy looked sheepish.

She shook her head. "Bloody hell, mate. Do you know how creepy and disconcerting that is for her? Marshall does the same to me—he's there every so often, watching. Outside my house or in Waitrose. Just happens to be in there to get his shopping at the same time as me—twice a week. He joined me in the cinema once and all. Sat in the row right behind me, and there wasn't a damn thing I could do about it."

"What?" Andy's eyes widened.

"Ah, so you can see how it is when it's happening to me, but you don't see the harm when it comes to Sarah, is that it?"

Andy blinked a few times. "Um, I didn't think of it that way."

"I bet. Listen, for whatever reason, you and Sarah split up. She's with someone else. It's been *years*—get over it. Move on. Find another woman. Be happy like her."

"I've tried with Louise Baker, but she's not interested."

"Maybe she will be now your smell problem is sorted." She cocked her head.

"Christ, I've really ballsed things up, haven't I." He stared at his Guinness.

"But you can fix it. Get yourself in better shape. Stop slobbing around. Clean your house so if you invite anyone over, they don't think you're a pig."

"Your punches sting, Stratton."

"They're meant to. Oh, here's our dinner, look. Shame I told them not to put the salad on, eh? You could have started as you meant to go on."

"Cheeky cow."

While the server placed their plates down, Helena studied Andy. She rarely glanced at him, not properly. In the past, the mere sight of him had her seeing red. But now, she looked at him as other people might, as if for the first time. He wasn't ugly, and his specs were trendy. He was a bit out of shape and could do with a haircut, but that wouldn't mean anything to the right woman. It was his demeanour. His take on life. Doom and gloom and then some. Maybe he was depressed and needed to see the doctor.

The server vanished after Helena thanked him, and she tucked into her meal, her stomach growling something chronic. Andy seemed to be enjoying his, attacking the peas first. Maybe her salad jibe had hit a sore spot and he was showing her he could eat the healthy bit instead of going straight for the salt-and-vinegar-soaked chips.

Halfway through, she paused. "I'll go to the gym with you, if you want." Where that had come from, she didn't know.

"When are we meant to fit *that* in when we're on a big case?" he asked.

"Right, that stops now."

"What does?" A speck of salt sat in the corner of his mouth.

"A negative answer right away. Think: I'll fit that in after work for an hour. Or: I'll get up early and go before work."

"You're fucking kidding me." He speared a square of steak he'd just cut off.

"Do you want my bloody help or not?" Helena rolled some chicken and salsa inside a wrap.

"I suppose."

"Good. So we'll go first thing. I'll pick you up at six. We can work out until seven-fifteen, and that gives us time to shower, eat, and get to the station by eight-thirty, all right?"

"But—"

She pointed at him. "Fuck off. We're doing it."

"Right."

"Right." She laughed. "It's for the best. A new you. New start. Then I won't have to put in for another partner, because you'll have got your act together."

"You what?" He frowned. "You'd actually do that?"

"Been thinking about it for ages." She shrugged then bit into her wrap. Christ, this chicken was lovely.

"I didn't realise. I just thought it was how we were. Bumbling along."

"Getting on each other's nerves…"

Andy grinned. "And that." He chewed on a chip. "Do you reckon we'll find our other halves?"

Helena had already found hers. Zach sprang to mind. When would they take the next step? After she'd had a word with Marshall about him loitering near her? She'd ring him later, when she got home. "This isn't about me. It's about you. But I'm telling you, if you don't lighten up, we won't be working together for much longer. I don't want to go and see Yarworth, but I will if I'm backed into a corner." She smiled at him to soften the blow. While she was being cruel, it was also to be kind. He needed this kick up the arse.

"I'll give it a go," he said. "You know, try my best."

"Good. That's a start, at least."

Helena finished her wrap and made another, some of the onions and a slice of red pepper hanging out of the top. The door beside her swung open, and she glanced across to see who'd come in. Jacob Walker ambled up to the bar and leant both elbows on it while he waited to be served.

"Ay up," Helena said, making eye contact with Andy and jerking her head to the right.

He turned that way. "Drowning his sorrows? People are allowed to get rat-arsed when their sister has died, you know."

"I know. Just saying. He lives two streets from me — saw it on the checks this morning. We'll need to speak to him tomorrow. There's something up with that family — did you feel it?"

"No." Andy rested his knife and fork on his plate.

"So you didn't notice how Suzie and Emma were a bit strange over the nails, mainly the polish?"

"Nope." He rubbed his temples. "I wasn't paying much attention, to be honest. Shit, I'm messing up all over the place."

"Oh, stop it with the negative bollocks, will you? Tomorrow, get on the ball. Listen, but specifically, watch. You *know* people give tells with body language. It's what they *don't* say that's important." She took a bite of food. Swallowed. "Both sisters were jittery over the nails. And Emma…didn't you clock it when she said, 'I should have said something'? She also said she didn't want to talk about it—about the red varnish."

"Um, again, no."

"What the hell were you doing during that interview? Head away with the fairies, was it?"

"Something like that."

"Well, that stops now, too, got it? Sharpen up your act. There's something dodgy about all this, and we need to find out what it is."

"Yes, boss." He gave her a wry smile, then, "Bugger it."

"What?"

"I just thought…"

"Careful, you might hurt yourself."

He huffed out a breath and attempted a smile. "I haven't got any sports clothes."

"Lord Almighty," she said, grabbing her wine. "Then buy some tomorrow, and we'll go the next day. I'm going to make a gym bunny out of you yet."

After another drink each, they walked back to Helena's, Andy calling for a taxi to meet him there in five minutes. Once she'd seen him off in it, she went inside and kicked off her shoes. Curled up on her sofa, she took a deep breath and, with alcohol fuelling her courage, she hit the Call button on her phone.

"Helena," Marshall said, all syrupy and far too sweet. "How are you, babe?"

She hated him calling her that. The hairs on the back of her neck stood at attention. "This isn't a social call. I'm ringing to warn you first, before I take it to the next level. Stop accidentally bumping into me, stop following me—don't deny it, I know you have—and stop hanging around outside my house. While you're at it, don't ring me. Now, I'm about to get a restraining order, so be prepared for that."

"What? We live in the same town. It's obvious I'm going to see you out and about."

"I'll give you that, but sitting behind me in the cinema, breathing down my neck? Standing on the other side of my street? Ringing me? That's not a coincidence. I'm a copper, Marshall. I know how these things go."

"You're up your own arse, you are. Like I'd want to follow a bitch like you around."

Helena's skin went cold. She wasn't going to bite. Really. "Fuck off, Marshall. This is your only warning." She cut the call and stared ahead at the picture on the wall above her fireplace. Concentrated on the brush strokes in the painting. Shaking—she was bloody shaking. And she wasn't about to convince herself it was from the cold. Deep down, despite how ballsy and 'with it' she appeared, she was like any other person in this situation—afraid of him and his temper. Now she thought about it, he was just like Uthway, the creep who'd locked her away in a metal storage container because she'd come too close to nicking him. He didn't feel anyone could tell him what to do or stop him from breaking the law.

Well, she was fucked if she'd let Marshall treat her like Uthway had.

No, he was going to learn to do as he was told.

CHAPTER SEVEN

Suzie sat beside Robbie on the sofa, staring into space while he watched some bullshit on TV. The kids were at his mum's. Betty had picked them up from school and said she'd have them for the night and take them to class in the morning. Suzie was grateful. She couldn't be doing with sorting them out at bedtime, not after spending most of the day in hospital and losing those wages. The lads were little monsters at the best of times, and she didn't think they'd cut her any slack despite what she'd been through. She had no energy to employ The Glare and The Voice this evening, so they'd have run rings around her.

Her chest was sore, but her heart more so, her eyes, too, from so much crying.

Callie. Gone. Just like Mum and Dad.

None of them had confessed to telling the truth, revealing the secret, when Dad had died while they'd been youngsters, or with Mum just a few short months ago. Suzie had come to the conclusion that Emma or Callie had said something both times, because Suzie had been too frightened to. *He* was an evil bastard and wouldn't think twice about doing as he'd said again. Three murders made that pretty clear. So far, he was sticking to *his* promise—if they breathed a word, he'd kill family members. First Dad, then Mum, and now Callie. Emma would be next, but if Suzie didn't say anything, her only remaining sister would be safe.

Emma wouldn't sign her own death warrant, would she?

Neither of them could risk opening their mouths. She'd have to speak to Emma in a bit and reiterate the warning, although, like Suzie, Emma didn't need a reminder, not with Callie dead.

Suzie thought about the gardening gloves, and a shiver scarpered up her spine on heavy size nines. It was a blatant clue left for her and Emma, but the police wouldn't have any bloody idea what it meant. Why did he have to *do* that? Just Callie being killed was enough. Adding salt to the wound with the clue was him all over, though. He enjoyed being in control, the sadistic bastard.

"You all right, love?" Robbie asked when the show broke for the adverts.

Suzie was jolted out of her thoughts and absently watched a woman on the screen showing the benefits of a cordless hoover. "Yeah, just tired."

"I don't mean about you blacking out." He reached over and squeezed her hand.

"I know what you meant. Still tired." Of all...this. Of what had happened and how it continued to control her life. At eighteen, she'd married Robbie quickly after a whirlwind romance—a good excuse to leave the family home with all the memories whispering from the walls. And going to bed with Robbie—like *that*—was nothing compared to how it'd been with *him*. The fact that *he* still insisted on being in her life was her cross to bear, something she'd put up with if it meant keeping Emma and Callie safe.

She winced.

I don't need to keep Callie safe anymore.

"I can't get over it," Robbie said. "You know, what happened to Callie, and so soon after your mum and all."

Mum's death had looked like a heart attack, but Suzie knew it wasn't. Mum hadn't had a

heart problem — not that they knew of anyway —
so he'd done what he'd said and killed her.

"Maybe we should move away." Christ, had
she said that out loud?

"If you like," Robbie said. "I'll go wherever
you go, you know that."

Yes, she did.

It was something to think about.

Emma had served pint after pint in The
Villager's Inn, and her arms ached. She was
dying for a fag, and her break time had long
since passed. She'd been too run off her feet to
take it. Now the customers had either buggered
off home or no longer lined the bar three deep,
she told the shift manager she was going for a
smoke.

She went out to the side of the pub and leant
against the wall, glad to be away from the hustle
and bustle indoors. It was bloody cold, and she
rubbed her bare arms, goosebumps springing up
beneath her palms. Sighing, she fished a
cigarette out then lit up, stuffing the packet and
lighter in her back jeans pocket. Her hand shook
as she raised it to her mouth for a long, calming
puff.

She'd spent the day after the police had left
mooching around her house, their lives and

unhappiness swirling inside her mind to the point she'd head butted the wall and left a dent. Harming herself was sometimes the only way she could cope. If she had that sort of pain to deal with, to concentrate on, the bigger, more devastating things faded somewhat. For a short while.

She should have visited Suzie in hospital but hadn't been able to face it.

She hadn't said a word about the secret this time, so it had to have been Suzie for Callie to be dead. Dad dying had been enough for Emma to keep everything locked up inside since she'd told him someone was fiddling around with his daughters. He hadn't even had a chance to get to work on the morning she'd let it all out. He'd promised to sort it once he got home, but on the way to his job at the bank, his car had swerved into a tree, and he'd apparently died on impact.

How had *he* known she'd told on him? He hadn't been around at the time—or she hadn't seen him anyway. How had he had the foresight to mess with the brake pads the way he had? How had he found the time? The police had said they were dodgy, but regardless of that, Dad's death had been put down to an accident.

But Emma knew better.

So had Callie.

So did Suzie.

So did *he*.

Her phone rang, and she sighed again, drawing it out of her front pocket and swiping the screen. Suzie was calling. Emma should have rung her way before now, or at least checked in with the hospital to see how she was doing, but it was all too much. This…this desecration of her family.

"Hi," Emma said. "Are you okay, Suz?"

"Yes, don't worry about that. It was just my stupid body doing a number on me. How are you?"

"Coping. I'm at work." Emma waited for the shriek.

One…two…

"What?" Suzie delivered.

Emma shrugged, even though her sister couldn't see it. "Better than being at home and thinking about…everything."

"True." Suzie sighed. "I'm sitting here wondering what the hell's gone on. I'm in the bedroom, obviously. I can't let Robbie know what it's all about. Not yet anyway."

What the fuck did *that* mean?

"I didn't say a word to anyone," Suzie went on. "Did you?"

"No, I swear I didn't. Why would I do that?" *Especially after I got our dad killed.* She'd learnt full well that opening her mouth brought terrible results—and had never admitted to her part in them losing him. It was too awful. She'd killed

Dad as much as *he* had. "I don't mean to sound horrible here, but Mum dying... Do you think that was Callie's fault?"

"Well, it bloody well wasn't mine." Suzie sounded well affronted.

"Nor mine. Fuck."

"Maybe Callie..."

Emma's heart pitter-pattered so hard her chest hurt. She drew on her cigarette. Could Callie have had enough to the degree she'd rather be dead? They all knew she was next on the list after Dad and Mum, so... Had Callie been so distraught about their childhoods that she'd no longer been able to carry on? Emma knew that feeling. It had lived inside her for years. "What, you think she told him she was going to say something, and he...?"

"Well, if it wasn't you or me..."

Emma took another pull on her fag. On the way out of her mouth, the smoke had her thinking about dragon's breath. With her finger, she traced her arm tattoo of a fire-breathing dragon standing in front of a castle with five turrets. "Then she must have. I hate blaming her when she's dead and can't defend herself."

"I know, but... Listen, I think we're going to move away. Robbie's on board with the idea. I can't keep living round here."

Emma almost choked. "You can't! You know what *he* said."

"I do, but what if you come with us? What if we all change our names and tell the police—"

"Fat lot of good that would do. And how are you going to explain a name change to your husband?" God, Suzie could be such a thicko at times.

"Well, we'd have to tell him everything. Without *him* around, we'd be safe to do that, wouldn't we? *He* wouldn't know where we were."

"No, it won't work, because he'd find us anyway, no matter if we have new names. You know what he's like. He'll come, then we'll be dead. I don't want to fucking die, Suz. Do you?"

"God, no. No! I can't leave the boys."

"Well then, we're stuck here, aren't we, in this shitty seaside town." Some days it seemed like even the sea knew their memories, and with each waft of the tide coming up the beach, the watery whispers rushed over the shingles, telling everyone on the shore what had happened. Emma had a thought. "And isn't that just convenient? We have tourists all year round. He can blame Callie's murder on that. Someone passing through. Some weirdo on a winter holiday just had the urge to bump a woman off."

"He would, too."

Emma bit her lip. "She rang me, you know. Last night."

"Callie?"

Emma tutted, irritation flaring. "Who else are we talking about here? Yes, Callie. She said someone was in the back garden. She got Nigel from next door to go round there and have a look, but there was nothing, no one. You know how many times she rang me claiming there was a man in the house—that *he* was in there. I brushed it off—couldn't get out of work to go to hers anyway, the boss was on and in a mood— and I should have gone there, because—"

"No. You are *not* going to blame yourself. If you didn't tell, if you didn't say anything about... Well, then it isn't your fault. Maybe it was *him* there all those times. Maybe he's changed the rules and hasn't told us. I wouldn't put it past him to go to hers and put the shits up her. He can hardly do it to me, what with having Robbie in the house."

Emma's stomach rolled over. "What if he does the same to me next?"

"Bloody hell, Em..."

Emma walked to the corner of the pub and glanced up and down the street, fearful he was hanging about and had heard her side of the conversation. Then she blurted, "Maybe it *was* Callie and he'd been going to her and frightening her as a warning. Then, when she kept saying she was going to open her mouth, he..." Emma hated that idea. *Hated it.* Why did she let her mind roam like that? Why did she let it all in, time and time again?

"It's all I can think of," Suzie said. "I know it wasn't me, and I believe it wasn't you."

"Same. Listen, I have to go." She couldn't stand talking about this shit any more tonight. "Are you at work tomorrow?"

"No, I'm having another day off. My chest is still tight. Plus, I rang my manager about Callie. Seems the staff already knew. The police have been there questioning everyone."

Emma felt sick. All those people, gossiping about their sister.

"Will you come round so we can discuss the funeral?" Suzie asked. "I don't even know how long they have to keep the body because she was…killed. And we still have to formally identify her, unless they'll take dental records as proof. Bloody hell, this is so horrible, Em. I don't want to see her. I don't think I can stand it."

"I know." Emma's eyes leaked, and she angrily swiped the tears away. She didn't want to see Callie either, especially knowing her mouth had been sewn up—another clue from him to them. With her mouth closed, she couldn't talk, and with her…her downstairs bits closed, she couldn't have sex. Was that what he was saying? That Callie could have no one but him? What about Emma in that regard? And why, then, was it okay for Suzie to be married to Robbie if he still wanted them all for himself?

"Are you still there, Em?"

"Yes. I just drifted off in my head for a minute, that's all. Okay, we'll get hold of the police and ask them what happens next. They might even contact us first."

"Right. Come round whenever. I don't have to take the kids to school, they're at Betty's tonight, so I'll be here anytime."

"Good. I'm in no mood to wrestle those buggers into class with you."

"Me neither."

"I love you, Suz."

"Love you, too, Em."

They said their goodbyes, and Emma sparked another ciggie. Fuck the consequences when she went back in to work. She thought about Ben and Toby, her devil nephews, and contented herself with the fact that they might be little sods, but at least they didn't have to endure what their mother and aunts had.

If *he* touched them, *she'd* fucking kill *him*.

Now there's a thought.

CHAPTER EIGHT

In the darkness, he sat on the kerb outside Emma's house and waited. The sea sounded rough, the swish and whoosh of it angry and violent. A bit like him. He needed to speak to her, to ensure she wouldn't say anything — make it clear that Suzie really would be next if they didn't keep their traps shut.

Emma had grown into a surly bitch, all that black and white she always had on, her house the same. She'd told him once that what he'd done meant she hated colours, that the only time she properly acknowledged them was in her dreams or when she thought about those fantasy lands she used to blether on about as a kid.

Weird cow.

She'd be here soon, shuffling up the street, her shoulders hunched with grief for Callie and hate for him. Well, he'd warned them all, time and time again, and they hadn't listened. Someone had told their dad. He'd heard the conversation and hadn't been able to make out which bitch it had been. And someone had blurted to their mum, what with her calling him to her place and asking questions. He'd bet it was Callie… Well, she'd basically killed herself in the end, the dozy bint. Her recent texts to him were meant to serve as proof for her to have evidence against him, it was well obvious, so he hadn't answered her in the way she'd clearly wanted. He'd replied that he had no idea what she was on about and she needed help; it was all in her head.

The only time he'd admitted anything was after he'd done a sweep of her house to make sure she didn't have any listening devices stashed away somewhere. She was batty enough to buy some. Paranoid, that was Callie. She should have known he'd have found them if there were any, so it was a good job she hadn't bothered using them, wasn't it.

He'd demanded to check her phone, too. If she'd been recording him, he'd have slapped her to kingdom come for that.

Last night, he'd stood in Callie's back garden for ages, staring up at her bedroom window, at the light on in there, a lamp placed beside the curtains on her posh girl's vanity table. She'd had ideas above her station, that one, always wanting to be better than everyone else. Promiscuous, she'd slept her way around town, and he'd heard all about it down the pub. Dirty slapper.

She'd said once that makeup was a mantle—that was exactly what she'd called it, a fucking mantle—and she draped it over herself, like some sort of superwoman cape, using it to help her get through because he'd ruined everything when they'd been little. He'd put bright-blue eyeshadow on her, and it had reminded him of the other woman he'd killed. She was the one who'd started all this, the old bitch.

Whatever. The girls he'd visited after he'd moved out of the family home hadn't gone off the rails like Callie, although he'd had to dispose of them once they'd shown signs of spilling the secret. Elsa, the new girl, now she thought it was great having a man as a boyfriend. He reckoned she'd be good for a few sessions yet. She'd keep her lips sealed and seemed to like him being nice to her. *She* didn't need a mantle.

He'd ripped Callie's nails off, had taken them home, and once all the flesh beneath them was dry, he'd paint them red.

He gripped the sewing kit to his chest. It was too soon to kill again, so it was a good job his kit kept him on an even keel, calming him. Just having it close, knowing what it represented, was enough.

The sound of scraping footsteps echoed, the time between them hitting the pavement long, as though the walker was too tired to put one foot in front of the other. He glanced down the street. There she was, Emma, moving along as if she had the weight of the world on her bony-arsed shoulders, head down, lost in her own world. She was probably thinking about those stupid dragons.

He stood and waited beneath a lamppost, sliding his sewing kit away in his inside denim jacket pocket. He couldn't wear the mac and the fedora so soon after last night. People might remember a man just like him wearing it around where Callie lived.

He cleared his throat, and Emma tipped her head back sharply.

She gasped and slapped a hand to her chest. "You!"

"Glad to see you remember me. I'm surprised you do. You haven't answered my last text, taken any of my calls, or opened the door when I've been round lately."

"I didn't want to," she snapped. "And is it any wonder?"

She was getting bold, this one. He'd have to take her down a peg or twenty.

Emma brushed past him, more vigour in her steps now, as if annoyance lent her speed. She stormed up her path. He followed her, and she went inside, turning to slam the door in his face. He stuck a foot out so she couldn't.

"Uh, no," he said. "We need to talk."

She stared at him defiantly, and he'd just bet she was thinking of telling him to go and fuck himself. He would, but it wasn't half as much fun on his own. She sighed and strutted off down the hallway, into the kitchen.

He went inside and closed the front door, slipping the safety chain across. Although he hadn't reckoned on doing anything tonight, things might go tits up, and plans might have to be changed.

You never could tell.

She was boiling the kettle, the old thing growling; the element was probably thick with limescale where she'd had it for so long. She jammed a round teabag in a black cup and spun to face him where he stood in the doorway.

"Say what you've come to say then get out," she said. "I've heard it all before, but I daresay I'll be hearing it a few more times in my future."

If she had a future, he'd agree, but either she or Suzie would balls it up and say something eventually — either to him or someone else — and then Emma would be gone, too.

He casually leant on the doorframe. "I don't think I need to say anything, do I? Three deaths says it all, really."

She narrowed her eyes at him, eyes that used to show fear but now just glittered with anger, pity, disgust, and a number of other things he didn't fancy contemplating. He shrugged it off as though it didn't matter *how* she saw him now. He didn't give much of a toss.

"Why did you sew her up?" Emma asked, her bottom lip quivering.

She always had got straight to the point, and oh, he hadn't expected the police to tell her that. He'd thought maybe they'd keep the gruesome details to themselves until they absolutely had to say something.

"You know why," he said.

"And Suzie having a blackout. Do you get off on all this or what?" Emma held a hand up. "Don't answer that. I don't want to know what goes through that sick head of yours." She turned side-on and poured steaming water into her cup, undoubtedly standing that way so she didn't have her back to him.

There was no telling what he might do, was there.

He hid a smile at that.

"Just make sure you keep your gob closed," he said, reaching into his pocket to stroke his sewing kit. "Then everything will be fine."

"I didn't breathe a sodding word, and Callie's still dead! Unless Suzie's lying to me and she—"

"No. She didn't."

"What then? Why did you do it? What's the point in forcing this secret on us if you're going to go against what you said and kill us anyway?" She spooned sugar out of an open bag of Tate & Lyle. Half of it slid off onto the worktop from her hand shaking.

Anger or fear?

"Callie did it to herself, the silly twat," he said. "She had a big mouth, your sister."

"What?" The spoon clanked into the sink beside her, and Emma stared at him, her mouth hanging open.

"She was going to tell. She told me as much."

"But she wouldn't have, you know that." Emma rubbed her forehead. "She was always saying things like that. Same as saying you were in her house in the middle of the night. It was all lies."

"Ah, but she didn't lie there. I *was* in her house. I liked watching her sleeping. It took me back to when she was a kid."

"Oh God, you're something else, you are."

"I know."

She *did* turn her back on him then but watched him in the kitchen window, their reflections fuzzy round the edges from the double glazing.

"I don't know what to say to you to make you see I won't talk." She pulled a packet of cigarettes out of her back pocket.

"Don't do that," he warned.

"My house, my rules." She put a fag in her mouth and lit it, sucking so hard her cheeks hollowed. Then blew the smoke over her shoulder in his direction.

Defiant bitch.

He closed his eyes momentarily to stop himself from lashing out at her. "But I'm the man in the house, so when I say don't smoke, you don't smoke."

"But you're *not* the man," she sniped, whipping round to stare at him, cigarette held high. "You never have been. I suppose you think you're the man of Suzie's house as well, don't you?"

"More so than her drip of a husband, yes." He took a step forward, the plastic case of the sewing kit sliding beneath his sweaty fingers. "I've always been the main man. The first man."

"You never gave us much choice with that, did you." She glared at him, spots of colour filling her cheeks. "And those gardening gloves. The nails on them. What the *fuck* did you do *that* for?"

Well, the police really had been free with the info, hadn't they.

"Just a little reminder," he said. "I have things like that in mind for both you and Suzie, and we all know I'll be leaving them behind once you're dead."

"What the hell happened to you to make you like this?" She shook her head, hatred skewing her features into a mask so she looked like her mother when she was annoyed.

That black eyeliner of hers had to go. It wasn't attractive at all. He didn't know what all those blokes she shagged were thinking, going with her. She'd ruined herself since she'd become an adult. She was nothing like the sweet-faced Emma of childhood.

"Stop wearing that shit on your face," he advised. "Callie learnt the hard way to ignore me about makeup. None of you need it."

"I'll wear what I damn well please." She stubbed her cigarette out in an ashtray then bent down to take milk out of the fridge. She added some to her cup, the carton wavering.

The cheeky cow hadn't made him one.

"You'll do as you're told," he said.

"D'you know what?" She paused and slammed the milk down. "Piss right off. I've had enough of this. Suzie was right. We should m—" She clamped her lips shut.

"You should what?" he asked, moving forward another two steps.

80

"None of your business." She went to pick the cup up.

He lunged forward and swiped it off the worktop. She squealed and backed away, staring from the broken cup and spilt tea on the black lino to his face.

"You don't want to get me angry," he said. "Or I'll—"

"Or you'll what?" she spat. "Kill me?" She chuffed out a bitter laugh. "Well, you're going to do it at some point, aren't you, so why not now?"

He tilted his head and regarded her.

Why not, indeed.

CHAPTER NINE

Helena sat in her office at lunchtime, munching on a cheese and pickle sandwich. She'd spent the morning on a wild bloody goose chase, trying to find Jacob Walker. He was a delivery driver for Waitrose—why did all the family work there except for Emma?— and each time she drove to his next drop-off, he'd been and gone. Andy had grumbled big-time at that, but she'd reminded him to switch his mindset to happy not grouchy. In the end, they'd phoned Jacob, and he'd said he'd be happy to have a chat with them after work. He finished at two and would come to the station.

Why is he at work at a time like this?

With no other leads, and nothing from Zach yet about Callie's PM, Helena had left Olivia and

Phil to poke about some more as well as sift through the doorstep interviews from the people in Callie's street. Phil had checked CCTV, but of course, there were no cameras on that part of the estate, only outside the row of local shops, and no one had appeared there or from the roads leading out of the estate, so they were shit out of luck. Helena had concluded the killer lived on the same estate or had tromped over the cliff top to get home.

A thousand or so houses. All those people to speak to. She thanked her lucky stars it was a job for the uniforms.

Andy was out at Sports Direct to pick up some gear. She'd been surprised and had thought he'd have called the whole gym thing off. Maybe their chat last night had sunk in after all.

Her desk phone rang, the red light for the front desk flashing. She picked up the receiver. "Hi, Louise."

"Hi, guv. I've had a call from a Suzie Walker, worried about her sister, Emma. Aren't they the sisters of the murder victim yesterday?"

"Yes. What did she say? Why is she worried?"

"Emma was supposed to be going round to Suzie's this morning, only she never turned up."

Fuck. This could either be nothing or…something. "All right. Leave it with me. I'll nip to Suzie's now. Thanks."

She put the phone down and thought about Andy chewing her arse if she didn't take him with her. He was right—she had to stop going places on her own and shutting him out. If he was willing to change, so was she.

Using her mobile, she gave him a ring.

"Yeah?" he said.

"Where are you?" she asked.

"Stuck in a long-arsed queue holding a pair of skin-tight workout bottoms, shorts, and a few tops."

She shrieked with laughter. "Skin-tight bottoms? What are you thinking of doing, going on bike rides? It's not Lycra by any chance, is it? Don't let Louise catch sight of you in it."

"Have I picked up the wrong thing?"

"Um, yes. Listen, all joking aside, I'm coming to pick you up. Suzie Walker's worried about Emma. Her sister," she added, in case he really had been away with the fairies yesterday and had forgotten her name.

"Oh dear."

"Exactly my thought. Let's hope no one has a grudge on the entire family, eh?"

"Okay. I'll quickly put the tighties back and get something else."

"You do that. Just regular trakkie bottoms will do. Ask the assistant for them, otherwise God knows what you'll buy."

"Righty ho. See you in a bit."

"Yep."

She slid her phone in her pocket, picked up the last bite of her sandwich, and stuffed it into her mouth. Leaving her office, she had a think on what Suzie's call could mean then swiftly shoved it out of her mind. She didn't need to think along *those* lines until she had to.

In the incident room, she said, "Ol, Phil, I'm going to grab Andy and visit Suzie Walker. She's rung in with a worry about Emma. Ol, can you do me a favour and widen the net in your searches? We need to know if any of the family had problems in the past. Go way back—for all we know, this could be aimed at their parents and someone's taking it out on the children. Far-fetched, perhaps, but you never know. Life is full of weirdness, isn't it. Phil, keep at it with the CCTV and house-to-house info. I know you've been over it already, but look again. Thanks."

She left the room and nipped down the stairs then out the back to her car. She drove the short way to town and headed to the retail park on the outskirts. Andy waited outside Sports Direct holding a massive bag. There was a damn sight more than what he'd said in there.

He got in the car and tossed the bag into the back.

"What the hell have you bought?" she asked. "The whole bleeding shop?"

"Very funny. I spoke to the assistant like you said. Need I say more?"

She headed towards Suzie Walker's place. "Ah, you were conned into buying...hmm, let me see. Trainers, Dri Fits, special socks..."

"How did you know?"

She blushed a bit.

"Oh, been caught like that yourself, have you?" he asked, chuckling.

"Maybe. Still, you'll look the part in the morning, so it's worth it."

"I'm going to feel a dick."

"Blimey, I hope you don't. Whoever the dick belongs to might not be happy about that."

"Smart arse."

"Better than being mardy."

"True." He sniffed. "We really are starting again, aren't we?"

"We are. We'll both give this partnership a good go, then if it doesn't work, we move on, no hard feelings." She swerved into a space outside Suzie's. "Right, let's get in there and see what the problem is."

Andy knocked on the door, and it opened almost immediately, as though Suzie had been at the window, watching for them to arrive.

"Come in," Suzie said.

They followed her to the kitchen, and thankfully, this time Andy hadn't poured a bottle of cologne all over himself, so the back door remained shut. They all sat at the table, and Andy got out his notebook, withdrawing a pencil from the spirals.

"What's the problem?" Helena asked.

Suzie sighed out a shaky breath. "Emma was meant to be here today. I assumed she'd have come this morning. We needed to talk about Callie's funeral amongst other things, and it'd be best done when my kids aren't here. They're a bit...noisy. Anyway, I rang her mobile and her landline, and she's not answering. I also rang The Villager's Inn, just in case she'd picked up a day shift to keep her mind off things, and she's not there either."

"Does she behave like this usually?" Helena asked. "You know, is she late at all as a rule?"

"No, she's very punctual." Suzie linked her hands and rested them on the table. "I've been trying to think if we agreed on a solid time, but I'm sure we didn't."

"Right, shall we go over to her house then?" Helena canted her head at Suzie and studied the woman's face.

Relief bled into her features, and her shoulders slumped. "Yes. I was going to go, but she lives too far for me to walk."

"You have a key?"

"Yes."

"Then come with us. I can understand why you'd be worried, given what happened to

Callie, but unless you know of a family grudge, it's highly unlikely to be anything sinister. Maybe she's asleep—unwell, say, and needed to stay in bed. Or she's grieving and just doesn't want to face the world today."

"Maybe."

"Okay." Helena checked the clock on the wall. "It's coming up to two now, so it's a bit close to picking up time at the school. Is there anyone you can ring to collect them for you again? Jacob? Oh heck... I was meant to be speaking to him this afternoon." She looked at Andy. "Will you give him a ring for me and apologise? Say we'll nip round his house later."

Andy got up to make the call in the living room, and Suzie pulled her mobile across the table and rang someone called Betty. Helena got up and walked to the kitchen sink. She stared out into the back garden. A pair of silver bikes stood propped against a shed at the bottom, and a swing set sat in the centre of the grass, the red paint faded to a lilac-pink from years under the summer sun. Washing flapped on a rotary line, mainly sheets and kids' clothes.

"My mother-in-law will get the boys," Suzie said. "Robbie can pick them up from hers later when he gets home from work."

"Where's that?" Helena turned from the window to face Suzie. She knew already but wanted to get Suzie chatting about him. Perhaps they could fit an interview in with Robbie after they'd seen Jacob.

"He's a forklift driver for the delivery warehouse."

"Does he like it?" Helena asked.

"It's a job." Suzie shrugged. "One we need. We're in a bit of debt. Well, behind on the bills."

Helena smiled. "Would anyone benefit financially from Callie's death?"

"I have no idea," Suzie said. Then realisation dawned. "If you think *I* did it for money, you're sorely mistaken. I doubt Callie had anything to leave. She worked in Waitrose, same as me, and rents that house. She used her portion of the money Mum left us to pay her rent way in advance and buy herself a car."

"I wasn't suggesting anything," Helena said. "It just occurred to me, that's all. It helps narrow down the suspects."

"I see." Suzie un-bristled and offered an apologetic tilt of her lips. "Sorry. I'm on edge."

"What did you spend your portion on?" Helena queried.

"Fixing the roof on this shithole. Look, can we go? I'm so worried about Emma."

"Come on then."

Suzie picked up a bunch of keys and her phone, and they walked past Andy in the hallway. Outside on the step, Helena took a deep breath of the cold air while Suzie shrugged on a coat.

The journey to Emma's didn't take long, and they all stood on the path outside her house, the wind coming in off the sea sneaking between the two houses opposite and buffeting them a bit. Suzie's hair swept all over the place, and she reached up to push it off her face and hold it back, fingers flat against her head.

"I'll go in first," Helena said, popping on gloves and booties then holding her hand out for the keys.

Suzie placed them in her palm, frowning. Then, once again, she got the gist. "You have those gloves on in case…"

Helena didn't elaborate. The woman had enough on her plate as it was. "Stay out here with DS Mald."

She unlocked the door, and a waft of spoilt meat smacked into her. Not good. She stepped inside, then closed the door behind her quickly, surprised Andy hadn't spouted protocol at her—them both needing to go inside together—but he'd remained silent, for once. His know-it-all persona seemed to have vanished since they'd been to the pub last night, and she'd mellowed as well.

She checked the living room. It was exactly as it was the last time they'd been here—tidy. And so black.

In the kitchen, she filed away the presence of a broken cup on the floor, the spilt drink long since dried up. The heating was on, so it had obviously helped soak up the moisture, although some parts were slightly tacky-looking. Had Emma been startled and dropped it? Or was it just an accident and she couldn't be bothered to clean it up, too infused with the lethargy of grief?

Helena took the stairs and got her bearings at the top. A door stood ajar, the covers on the bed neat and tidy, so either Emma had slept in it and made it earlier this morning, or she hadn't slept in it at all. A spiral of unease unwound in Helena's belly, and she went into the room to open the wardrobe doors and lift the bed skirt to look beneath. Nothing but clothes in the former and dust bunnies on the carpet under the latter.

She checked two of the other closed doors—an airing cupboard stacked with sheets and towels and a small bedroom used as an office, a treadmill to the right. Outside the other door, she steadied her nerves. The swirl of dread in her gut intensified, and she had a horrible feeling she wouldn't like what was on the other side. A tangy aroma she'd smelled before gave her a massive clue, and she swallowed the lump in her throat, butterflies prancing about in her chest.

She twisted the knob and pushed the door open.

Emma was in the bath.

Helena would have liked the woman to shriek at being disturbed and caught naked, but Emma remained silent.

"Oh, fucking hell," Helena whispered and checked behind the door. There was only a toilet. She returned her attention to Emma.

The poor thing appeared to be asleep, having a nice relax, except there wasn't any water, only blood. She was covered in it, her belly gaping open, her innards on show. There was some kind of tattoo on her arm, but Helena couldn't make it out because of all the red stuff. A pink tulip stood in the centre of the foot-long hole in her gut, as though it grew out of her wrecked body, the soil the stabbed remnants of her liver.

The smell and sight, overpowering, had Helena gagging, and she breathed through her mouth and tasted the damn stench instead. She closed her eyes for a few seconds, still seeing Emma in her head. Gathering courage to look at her again, she cracked her eyes open a little.

Emma's mouth had been sewn up, this time with multi-coloured thread, so many shades it was mad to try to count them all. Her blood-streaked arms were by her sides, and her nails had been ripped off, the finger ends drying out, the blood brown and crusty there.

She'd been dead for a while then.

Helena dared to peer down *there*, and Emma had been closed up with the same thread, her hairs completely shaved off. A yellow rubber duck perched on her thighs where they met. This was a message Helena didn't understand. The mouth, yes—that was to say 'be quiet', but the vagina, the duck? She shook her head, not getting how someone had it in them to do this to another human being, and turned away to walk out and regain her equability on the landing.

"Helena?" Andy yelled.

She jumped and peered down the stairs. The letterbox was open, and the tips of Andy's fingers poked through.

"The house is clear, but I haven't checked the loft," she called and made her way downstairs to crouch at the door. "Andy?"

He hunkered down and peered at her, her visual just his eyes surrounded by his specs.

"Take Suzie to the car, all right?" she whispered.

He must have winced—his eyes scrunched up.

"I'll ring for SOCO and Zach," she said.

Andy blinked several times, then his face disappeared, as did his fingers, and the letterbox snapped shut, the clatter loud and so final, as though it wanted to mourn its owner's passing by slamming.

Helena stood and stared down the hallway to the broken cup on the kitchen floor.

What the fucking hell were they dealing with here?

CHAPTER TEN

*T*he camping event in the garden was a practise
run for when they did the real thing in St Ives on
the annual family summer holiday. Callie couldn't
wait to go all the way to the seaside – one that had
sandy beaches instead of the pebbles in Smaltern –
and it was 'dahn sarf' as Dad had said, instead of
being 'oop norf' where they lived. The weather would
be grand down there, the lady travel agent had
informed them, especially in August, and Callie
looked forward to digging her toes in the hot sand and
making castles, maybe even getting buried so only her
head showed.

It was late-April, the weather spring-like, a lovely,
warm sun but with a bit of a nip to the air when a
breeze soughed through. Still, it beat the harsh winter
they'd just had any day, with its stinging winds

smacking into the cliffs, sailing upwards then over to chill everyone in town to the tips of their toes. There had been quite a frost, too, which had rimed the grass and gathered at the edges of windows, and it looked perpetually Christmas each time Callie had stared outside through the glass.

They had a massive tent, family-sized. Dad had borrowed it from a work colleague, and they were going to camp in it tonight in the back garden. Inside the tent was a central area where Dad said they'd set up a table and chairs for eating at when on their actual holiday, and three bedrooms were offshoots at the back.

Some friends were going to St Ives at the same time – well, friends of Mum and Dad anyway. They had kids, too – three boys who were loud and annoying, and Callie was glad Jacob would be off dealing with them. She'd hang out with her sisters. It was going to be great.

Come bedtime on the test camp night, everyone snuggled inside sleeping bags on blow-up beds that creaked and wheezed with every movement. Sleep didn't come easily – they were all too excited – but in the end, after Suzie told fairy tales about dragons and castles, they all drifted off.

A strange sound woke Callie, though, a low hum, metallic. She sat up in the pitch-black and looked around, disorientated for a moment, forgetting where she was. A gap appeared in the zippered doorway to their bedroom section, and someone, a shadow, stepped through. Callie's breath caught in her throat, and she opened her mouth to scream, but the shadow's hand slapped over it, silencing her. It felt like whoever it was had a glove on, rough like those ones Mum used when pruning the rose bushes out the front.

The shadow whispered in Callie's ear, telling her things she never thought she'd hear, and her first session began.

CHAPTER ELEVEN

Helena met Zach on the pavement outside Emma's house. She took off her gloves and dropped them in an empty cardboard box for that purpose beside the gate, then rubbed her temples. A headache was coming on, nagging at the top of her neck and threatening to navigate to her crown.

Zach stood beside her in silence, concern stamping lines into his forehead. She smiled to let him know she was all right and dropped her hands to her sides, taking in the street to gauge how easily the killer could have been seen arriving then leaving. That gap between the two houses opposite — he could have run down there and walked along the cliff, and unless someone had been looking out and had spotted him, he'd have got away scot-free.

A few neighbours were nosing in what they probably thought was a surreptitious manner from their windows, or blatantly in their front gardens, some standing on tiptoes, leaning against garden gates and craning their necks to try to get a good gander inside the house. Emma's door was ajar, and Helena gestured to the black-haired policewoman on the step to close it a bit more.

"So it's Callie Walker's sister, you said?" Zach opened the passenger-side door of his car for Helena to get in.

"Yes."

"We may as well chat in here again while SOCO get the first bits done."

"All right." She got comfortable and waited for him to join her.

He climbed in and rubbed his hands together. "So cold out today."

"Hmm. We're meant to be getting the tail end of a bloody hurricane in the next few days."

"Marvellous. As if we don't get battered by the coastal winds enough as it is. The side of my house'll be buggered soon from the sea salt and weather." He paused. "Did you get hold of *him*, by the way?"

Zach didn't have to say the name for her to know exactly who he referred to. Bloody

Marshall. Helena glanced across at him. "Yes. He basically denied following me, of course — I'd expected that sort of bollocks. I warned him a restraining order would be on the way, but I suspect he thinks I'm joking. I'm expecting dog shit to be posted through my letterbox or something equally as unimaginative in retaliation, but who knows, maybe I'll be proved wrong."

"He'd better not try anything. Bit stupid if he does." Zach scratched his head. A tic beat in his jaw.

"Like I said to him, I'm a copper. I can deal with it." *I hope. It's a bit different when it's personal.* "He'll find some other poor cow to put up with him before long, I'm sure. He's a good-looking bastard, so someone will take him on, then regret it like I did. He's got all the charm, says all the right things at first, then a couple of months in, he changes. I've never met such a manipulative, childish, narcissistic person in my life." *Barring Uthway. Mustn't forget him.*

Like she ever could.

Zach cleared his throat. "Do you fancy a drink later then, now everything's sorted? Or sort of sorted."

He raised his eyebrows and appeared so worried about her answer; she didn't have the heart to turn him down. And she wanted this — had wanted it long before she'd started seeing

Marshall, if she were honest, but Zach had been with Kirsty back then, so Helena had kept her feelings to herself until Zach had dropped hints about his relationship with Kirsty going down the pan, him saying he'd be finishing it soon. And he'd done that, keeping a respectable emotional distance from Helena yet flirting a little to let her know he was available to her. She hadn't dared believe what she'd been hearing, so until yesterday hadn't let herself hope they could be together.

And here they were, discussing their first date, except it hadn't been laid out as a date. A meet-up in a pub under the guise of colleagues getting together, that was what it sounded like to her.

"That'd be nice." She had to get any crossed wires laid out straight in nice neat rows so she knew where she stood. "A date, is it?"

"Of course," Zach said on a laugh. "What else did you think it was?"

"I don't know."

"Hey, I might even spring for dinner. You don't even have to go Dutch."

She smiled. "The Blue Pigeon near my place? They do lovely food. I ate there last night with Andy."

"Really?"

"Yes." She rushed on, so he didn't think anything weird was going on. "We're working through some kinks in our partnership."

"Um, I don't want to know about that sort of thing. Kinks." He winked when she gasped and swatted his leg. "I'm joking. I know what you meant. Will eight o'clock do you?"

"Yes, that's fine. I'll meet you there. So..." She had to change the subject before her fluttering stomach had her being sick from excitement. "Emma Walker. Clearly, it's someone who has a grudge against the sisters—we've already arranged for Suzie and her family to be placed elsewhere until we find who did this, and Jacob, the brother, has also been relocated, just in case. They're in flats next door to each other so they can support one another—ground floor, which isn't ideal, but it's better than nothing. As for Emma..." Helena sighed, remembering the state of the woman, and she batted the thought away of whether she'd been in immense pain or had been knocked unconscious before she'd been killed. Helena could only hope for the latter. "She's in the bath. She's been sliced from just under her breasts down to her belly button. There's a tulip sticking out of the mess of her stomach."

Helena's eyes watered, but she wasn't going to knuckle the tears away. Zach reached out a hand and took one of hers. The touch was a comfort but also dangerous. It took her mind right off Emma and straight to other things—things she shouldn't be thinking while at work. If she wasn't careful, Zach could derail her determination on the job, have her head spinning until she couldn't think straight.

He seemed to sense that was the case and drew his hand away, resting it on his lap.

"Roses on the gardening gloves, a tulip with Emma…" he said.

Helena could have kicked herself. "You're right." Then, as if she wanted to soothe the sting of not noticing that for herself, she said, "It might be nothing, though."

"But it might be everything. Listen, I know you don't like talking about Uthway, but look at what he did. Those clues he left were so obscure, yet once you found out what they meant, they made sense. Maybe Suzie and…Jacob, is it? Maybe they'll understand the significance."

"There's something off about the nails—specifically nail polish," she said.

"You're telling me…"

"What do you mean?"

"I'll talk about that in a minute. Carry on."

Helena wanted to know now, damn it, but did as he'd asked. "I'd intended to question Emma about it again today after I'd spoken to Jacob, but that's off the table. She's dead, and I can't speak to Jacob until later once I've finished here. But you're right. If it's a family thing, they might know."

"You'll get to the bottom of it. You always do." Zach blew out a breath, and the faint scent of his aftershave wafted over.

It did mad things to her.

"Suppose we'd better go in then," she said. "Before we do, though, tell me what you meant. Have you done Callie's PM yet?"

He nodded. "This morning. I was about to write up my report and email it to you when the call came in to come here. Definite strangulation. Bruises came out overnight, mainly on the torso, the belly area, as though she'd taken a few punches there. Fingerprints on the arms, where someone perhaps gripped her. And…um…I found things inside her."

Helena's stomach lurched for an entirely different reason this time. She closed her eyes for a moment, dreading what she was about to hear. Had Callie been drugged? Was her liver pickled, her kidneys damaged? "Go on."

"A bottle of red nail varnish in her mouth and an artificial red rose—just the flower—in her vagina."

"What?" She stared at him, mouth hanging open. She hadn't expected… What *had* she expected? Was that the only reason Callie had been sewn up, to keep those items inside? Helena's first instinct that it showed Callie was now kept quiet forever and could no longer have sex might be defunct. "Bloody hell…"

"I know. A first for me. This is the most deranged thing I've had on my table since the Uthway case. I thought bodies being carved with ancient symbols bad enough, but this feels like it's a different level somehow. More personal."

"I agree. Someone in that family has got to know the significance. I'll have to push Suzie and Jacob—or maybe Robbie, Suzie's husband, knows something." She sighed out through pursed lips. "You should know…Emma's been sewn up as well."

"Then my guess is there will be items inside her, too."

"Fuck." She slammed her head back on the seat. "Come on. I'll go inside with you for a bit, then I need to get on. Andy will be wondering where I am. I left him guarding the bathroom door. I wanted her kept safe, for someone to be there with her, not just left like that…" Her eyes itched. She nodded at the windscreen. "Uniforms are here. House-to-house enquiries— let's hope something comes to light and the neighbours weren't all in bed. I assume it happened during the night. The heating was on when I went in, so it might cock up your time of death estimate."

"I'll get a general idea. Did she seem in rigor?"

"Hard to tell—and that wasn't a pun. I was too busy taking in the state of her. And the duck."

"The duck?"

"Yes, she has a yellow rubber duck on her legs."

"What the actual fuck?"

"I know. It'll mean something, I just don't know what at the minute."

Zach sighed. "Let's go in."

They left the car, and while Zach put his whites on then went inside, Helena chatted to the officers who'd arrived. She reminded them what types of questions to ask the residents, feeling a bitch for doing so when they were already well-versed, but wanting them to understand how important it was to get the right answers. "Make sure you grill them well—as you probably know, this is the second murder, but what you might not know is they're sisters. We need to find this wanker in case the killer is after the other two siblings as well."

Regardless of the fact that Suzie and Jacob were in safe houses, the murderer might have been hanging around and watched them being escorted there. Although officers would have done their best to get the family to safety without being spotted or tailed, sometimes it didn't work that way.

Mistakes happened.

She left the uniforms to it, put on fresh gloves and blue booties, and entered the house. The smell of Emma's blood and guts hit her straight away, and it seemed stronger than when she'd first arrived—maybe because the scent clung to the insides of her nostrils now and the bathroom door was open. She turned the heating off at the temperature dial, asking the female constable outside the door to note down the time Helena had done it. A click came from the boiler upstairs, and she climbed the steps and stood in the bathroom doorway.

"I'm going out for some fresh air," Andy said.

"I don't blame you."

He tromped away.

Someone had put a transparent plastic sheet on the floor, and Zach knelt beside the bath. He had a packaged thermometer in his gloved hands, opening it. Helena turned away while he used it. The sight of him inserting it into Emma's backside wasn't something she wanted embedded in her memory.

"Give or take an hour or two, what with the heating being on, I'd say she died after midnight, three a.m. at the latest," Zach said. "You can look now."

Helena did, her sight landing on that rubber duck with blood spatter on its orange beak. Her guts churned, and she took a deep breath through her mouth in an attempt to calm her racing heart.

"Do you want me to check what's in her mouth and down below now?" he asked.

"Go on then, so long as you're happy to do it."

"I'm never happy to do anything like that."

"You know what I meant."

"I do. Right then…"

He took a pair of clippers out of his black bag and snipped at the rainbow thread on Emma's lips.

Helena turned and waved at a SOCO in the main bedroom. "Can we have a couple of evidence bags here, please."

"I'll get them," Tom said, poking his head around the doorframe.

"Ooh, I didn't know you were in there. Hello," she said.

"All right?"

"Okay, considering."

"Grim, this," Tom said, coming to stand beside her.

Zach held out the multi-coloured thread, and Tom stepped forward, opened a bag, and Zach dropped the cotton inside. While Tom sealed the bag and wrote on it, Helena gave Emma her attention.

"Rigor is almost gone, so it shouldn't be too much trouble," Zach said. He prised the mouth open and peered inside.

Something black and round rested between Emma's teeth. Zach used grips to take hold of it and pulled it out. A bottle of pink nail varnish — the black circle was the top of the lid.

"Christ," Helena said. "Another bag, please, Tom." She frowned hard. "What the *hell* does it mean?" She didn't expect an answer; it just helped saying it out loud.

"Right, now we'll see what else we have," Zach said.

Tom went off to get another bag while Zach clipped at the thread between Emma's legs.

"Get two," Helena called to Tom. "That duck is pissing me off, staring at me like that."

Tom brushed past her and went into the bathroom, popping the offending item into a bag. He stood to the left and wrote in the white boxes with a Sharpie.

Zach held out the second thread, and Tom took it. Helena looked at the floor while Zach parted her legs. Some things were just too harrowing to see. This poor woman had been alive and well yesterday, distraught over her sister's death, and now, here they all were, standing over her. She'd become evidence, nothing more, a shell, something they inspected to work out who'd killed her. She wasn't Emma Walker who'd once laughed and sang and cried and got angry.

It was sickening, what these bodies were reduced to.

"Err, it's not a flower," Zach said.

Helena snapped her head up. "Maybe the tulip in her stomach is all we're going to get in the flower department. Actually, Tom, can you get rid of that as well? The tulip, I mean."

"I'll just go and get a bigger bag." He left the room.

"Dare I ask what's in there?" Helena needed to know, but it didn't mean she wanted to. Jesus, this was all so…so hideous.

Zach eased the item out. He held it up with a large pair of tongs.

Helena's legs almost gave out. She couldn't comprehend what she was seeing. Blinking, she focused on what it was, but the main thing that bothered her was why it had been placed inside her. What did it *mean*?

"I don't get this at all," she whispered.

"Me neither."

Helena couldn't stop staring at it. "Why would anyone put a man's electric shaver inside somebody?"

"I have no clue," Zach said. "And that's something you're going to need to find out."

CHAPTER TWELVE

*E*mma shared a bath with Callie most nights, but
Callie wasn't well and had gone to bed early, so
Emma had jumped in after Suzie and enjoyed a
splash about by herself. She still played 'witches',
where they pretended to be old crones, using the soap
to cast a spell over all the bubbles until they vanished.
The water turned milk-white, and Mum always
griped about how the bar of soap went down so
quickly, week after week, and who the hell was using
it that much for it to disappear so fast?

The door was ajar — Mum said they weren't old
enough to shut it or lock it yet. Emma would have to
get out soon. She was turning into a prune. It'd be
Jacob's turn in a bit, and he always had clean water,
then Dad usually got in afterwards. Mum preferred a
shower, and she had that later, just before bed once

the water heater had done its job and warmed another tankful.

Emma rested back, gripping the silver handholds either side so she could float and pretend she was swimming. Soap scum created a ring at water level, and she'd have to remember to give it a wipe with the flannel once she'd finished.

She closed her eyes, and something nudged her leg. She peeked. The yellow rubber duck bobbed along, hovering over her legs. Callie usually played with it – Emma was too old for that sort of thing now. Or that was what she told her friends anyway.

Letting her eyes shut again, she imagined she was in the sea, sand under the water and not the pebbles round here that hurt her feet every time they went down to the beach for a picnic some Saturdays. Something touched her leg for a second time, and she smiled, thinking the duck was coasting along again. Whatever it was moved up her thigh and pressed between her legs, and her heart pattered a little; she sensed something was wrong.

She snapped her eyes open, and he was there, looming over the bath, although he was on his knees. His hand was where it shouldn't be, and she opened her mouth to say so, but he lifted a finger to his lips. He was tall and brawny, and he scared her, always did, but Mum and Dad said he was just a tad brusque and to take no notice, he didn't mean any harm.

Then he told her if she didn't keep this a secret, he'd kill her family, and her, so she nodded and let him do what he wanted, shaking all the while, not daring to make a noise as she cried.

"Next time I'll leave you a pink tulip outside your bedroom door," he said. "Men do that, see, give women flowers. And the next day, after our sessions, you'll put pink nail polish on, just so I know you're telling me you'll keep our secret. Every time you see your flower, I'll visit you."

Emma thought of the forget-me-nots she'd seen beside the doorjamb last week. Were they for Suzie or Callie? Suzie, she decided, because she'd been wearing purple nail varnish recently.

It was all so confusing and wrong, but he said it was right, it was what they should be doing, so she supposed, if Suzie was allowing it, then Emma would, too.

Afterwards, when he'd gone, she got out of the bath and wrapped herself in a towel, lost inside her head, the memory of what he'd done and said swarming into her mind and eddying, much like the water going down the plughole.

Jacob came in, and she jumped.

"Get out of the way so I can have a bath," he said.

Emma scuttled to the bedroom, and Suzie asked what was wrong.

"Nothing," Emma said. She didn't want anyone to die, and he was so mean, she believed he'd do it. Kill. Take away everyone she loved.

She got into bed, thinking she hadn't cleaned the scum, and Jacob would say something about it at the breakfast table in the morning.

After a few years, the brawny one handed her Dad's electric razor and told her to shave off her just-growing hair down below. He said he didn't like it, and if he ever caught her with any, he'd rip it out with his bare hands.

Emma obeyed.

For a while.

CHAPTER THIRTEEN

In the car on the way to the safe house flats, Helena couldn't get the sight of Emma out of her head. The image of her in the bath seemed stuck there, hovering, with no intention of buggering off anytime soon. While she'd be able to get the stench of death out of her nose and could carry on as if she'd never smelled it — until another ravaged corpse came her way — the same couldn't be said for memories. They lingered, fucked you up if you let them. She should know. Uthway's face floated in her dreams most nights. It even crept into day-to-day life, him seeming to appear in crowds or as extras on TV — the random man at the bar in *Eastenders* nursing a pint or a market trader out in The Square. "Roll up, roll up!" Except the

117

only rolling up Uthway did was putting bodies inside rugs and throwing them off the cliff.

He'd never go away, that one. He'd always be there, infecting her mind, a poison that infiltrated.

"That was a sodding rotten experience," Andy said. "Whoever this is, they're sick in the damn noggin."

"Going round your head, too, is it?" she asked, turning a corner and checking her rearview in case the killer had been hanging about outside Emma's and had it in mind to follow them. She wouldn't put it past the deranged shitbag to be watching them, revelling in what he'd done.

"It's hard *not* to think about it," Andy said, scrubbing a hand down his face. He sounded tired, worn out from the investigation already.

I know the feeling.

"It goes without saying, but we need to catch this fucker pretty sharpish," she said, swallowing a lump in her throat. The damn thing hurt.

"Easier said than done—we have no leads," Andy said. "When I went outside for a bit of air, I asked one of the uniforms how house-to-house was going, and can you believe out of the ones questioned, no one saw or heard anything?"

"Well, yes," she said. "It was after midnight. Most people were asleep."

"So Emma didn't scream, then, is that what we're to believe? Same as with Callie? No one heard them cry out, so they either didn't, or all the neighbours sleep like logs. Did he gag them first or what?"

"We'll find out from the PMs. Zach hasn't sent the report yet, but if there are fibres in their mouths, we'll know about it soon enough. I've got something to tell you. It's not pleasant, so you might want to brace yourself."

"What for?"

She told him what had been found inside Callie, cringing at how awful it sounded, how warped and wicked. Depraved.

"You what?" Andy shoved a hand through his hair. "What the hell is it with the flowers and the nail varnish?"

"Your guess is as good as mine." She checked the mirror again. Nothing, not even a pedestrian or someone out on a bike. "But you can bet it's important to the killer."

"Obviously, otherwise they wouldn't be leaving it there. I thought sewing their mouth and...you know, their... I thought that was weird enough."

"I don't understand it, I really don't—the items." She indicated to go left. "Okay, we know some people have the urge to kill, and I get that, I do. Spouses killing their abusers, people in love triangles, crimes of passion—I understand how that red mist can come down and change you into someone you never thought you'd be." She wished she'd killed Uthway, but you couldn't have everything, could you. "But to sew someone up, to do what was done, to leave weird clues... Callie was strangled — is that tied to her in some way? Emma...she was gutted. I didn't see any strangulation marks, did you?"

"No. Got to be a special kind of bastard, he has."

"Exactly. And that duck is bugging me. And as for the shaver..."

"Shaver?"

"Um, sorry, I was getting to that. It was found inside Emma, in her vagina. She had pink nail varnish in her mouth."

Andy blew out an extra-long breath. "Fuck me." He gazed through the side window, then turned to look at her.

She stared back for a moment, catching a dawning realisation in his eyes, then faced the road again. "What?"

"They match."

"What do?" She glanced in the mirror and, with no one behind, pulled up to the kerb outside the flats.

"The flowers and the polish. Red for Callie, pink for Emma."

"So they do." Helena switched the engine off and removed the key. "Suzie's *got* to know something, don't you reckon? I'm not buying her saying it means nothing to her."

"Maybe she really doesn't. It might just have something to do with the other two. Suzie's married with kids — she's not likely to be mixing with people, not with having nippers and a job to boot. Emma and Callie were single — Emma worked in a pub, plenty of chances to bump into a weirdo. They could have got messed up in some sex den or something."

"What, *here*?" Then she thought about that. Smaltern was the perfect place to run a sex den, what with the many outlying houses, some owned by the rich who might have a penchant for the unusual. Those big houses were private, closed in by tress and gates. Then there was the house in Lime Street where Uthway had kept people captive. "I seriously hope not. We'd have no clue where to start looking for people who were involved in such a thing."

"We did it with Uthway, so we'd do it again."

"Right, we should get in there and ask some questions. Suzie first, I think. She'll have her boys to sort later, so us hanging around at bedtime probably won't be appreciated."

They left the car and entered the block of flats. A PC stood in the hallway outside two doors at the end of the corridor, and Helena nodded at him.

"Let us in then, Clive, there's a dear," she said. "Everything okay?"

"Yes, guv, except some shopping's been delivered—Jacob Walker got one of his work colleagues from Waitrose to do it under the guise of helping an old woman."

That got Helena's back up. What an absolute dick. "I'll have a word with him and make him see the importance of not speaking to anyone while they're here. If he hadn't used the old lady excuse, I'd have been royally hacked off." Helena shook her head at Jacob's stupidity.

"I read him the riot act earlier," Clive said quietly, tilting his head in the direction of the second door, presumably where Jacob was. "He seemed suitably sorry."

"It was still a stupid thing to do."

"I took their phones away for now and all," Clive said, "seeing as he can't be trusted. I rang their bosses. Said they wouldn't be in because of two deaths in the family."

"Thanks for doing that. You're a star, mate." Helena smiled.

Clive used a key and pushed the door open. "I don't know if I like that. I don't fancy twinkling."

Helena laughed. "Shut your face, you."

She stepped inside, Andy at her heels, and called, "Suzie? It's Helena Stratton and Andy Mald."

Helena walked into the living room. A man—Robbie, she guessed—slouched beside Suzie on the sofa, and two young boys sat on the floor doing a large jigsaw.

"I'm so terribly sorry for your loss, again," Helena said, having been unable to say so when she'd discovered Emma. Suzie had been in the car, and once other officers had arrived, she'd been taken off-scene.

"I can't believe they're gone," Suzie said, her voice meek.

Christ, she looked a state, which wasn't surprising. Her eyes appeared sore, and her eyelashes clumped together where they were wet. She clutched a ratty tissue.

"Can we have a word in the kitchen?" Helena jerked her head towards the children, indicating what she had to say wasn't for their ears.

"I'll stay with the boys," the man said. "I'm Robbie, by the way."

He didn't seem too hot either. Helena reckoned he'd had all the stuffing knocked out of him. What a terrible thing for them all to go through. She wouldn't wish it on anyone.

Except Uthway…

"Right, come on then," Helena said and led the way to the kitchen.

Andy and Suzie joined her, and they all sat at the small pine table, the door closed.

Andy got up again, as if uncomfortable being so close to a grieving woman. "Tea or coffee?"

"Tea for me," Helena said.

"Coffee, please, although even having something as simple as that feels wrong," Suzie said. "Like I can drink it and my sisters can't. Oh God…" She barked out a sob.

"It'll get easier, I promise," Helena said, reaching out to squeeze her hand. "What I can't promise is you forgetting, because that will never happen, but you'll smile again, believe it or not, and laugh, and the first time you do, you'll feel guilty, but as time moves on, you'll perhaps learn to remember them fondly and not how they died or why. Do you *know* why?"

A doe about to scarper into the safety of the woods, caught in the sights of a hunter, that was what Suzie looked like.

"No." She shook her head. "No, I don't have any idea."

"Now," Helena said, the growl of the boiling kettle a backdrop. "I'm going to tell you something disturbing, and it's vital that if you know what it means, you tell me, understand?"

Suzie nodded, eyes wide, although she didn't seem too convincing at playing an innocent person.

What is she hiding?

"This will be hard to hear, okay, but I have to tell you because, to be honest, we have absolutely *nothing* to go on. Normally, we'd opt to keep this sort of thing to ourselves, but this person needs to be caught, and if what I say jogs your memory, it may well lead us to finding them. We're worried you and Jacob will be next, hence you being moved here." Helena took in a long breath then let it out slowly. "Callie and Emma had their mouths and vaginas sewn up."

"Oh shit..." Suzie slapped a hand to her forehead, and her eyelids fluttered as if she might faint.

"Deep breaths. That's it." Helena rubbed the back of Suzie's hand. "Are you okay for me to go on? Do you have your inhaler?"

Suzie closed her eyes. "Yes. In my pocket."

"The person who killed them put things in their mouths and private parts."

"*What*? I don't understand..." Suzie took her inhaler out and had a puff.

"All right for me to continue?"

"Yes."

"Callie had a rose and nail varnish inside her. Both red."

An animal sound crawled out of Suzie, half growl, half snarl. "Oh God... And Emma? Oh, my poor baby sisters. I can't... I want to say som..."

"Take another deep breath, love," Helena said.

"Emma had a pink tulip on her person, and inside her was pink polish and a man's electric shaver."

"What? A shaver?"

It wasn't lost on Helena that she hadn't had the same confused reaction about the varnish and the flowers. "Do you know what those items mean?"

The shake of her head came too quickly, too forcefully. This woman was keeping something to herself, Helena was certain of it.

"Why do you think a killer might want to leave those behind?" Helena pushed.

"I…I don't know."

"I'm going to take a punt and say you do, Suzie. You know what they're in relation to. Maybe not the shaver, but the flowers and the varnish…yes, you know. Emma knew, too. That much was obvious when we spoke to her yesterday but, like you, she wouldn't say. She said she didn't want to talk about it, which indicates there was something to talk *about*. Red roses and polish for Callie, a pink tulip and polish for Emma. Do you have a flower and polish, Suzie?"

Christ, have I gone too far?

"No. No, I don't. What a ridiculous thing to say." She sucked on her inhaler and closed her eyes.

Can't bear to let me see the lies in them?

"Okay. If you're frightened, if you've been threatened, you can tell me, and I will keep you safe, you know that, don't you?"

Suzie nodded, eyes still shut. "I can't..."

"You can."

"No, I can't." Her answer was strident this time, and she glanced around the room, gaze landing on the door. An escape route—get me out of here.

"That'll do for now. Take your coffee and sit with your boys. And have a think about whether the killer will come for them next." Low blow, but what the hell.

Suzie flinched and got up, walking to the door.

"Can you send Robbie in, please?" Helena asked, turning to look at her.

"Robbie?" Suzie's mouth dropped open, and she darted her gaze around, as though the walls were closing in, pressing on her. "What do you need to speak to him for?"

"Standard procedure. We speak to all family members. Friends. Acquaintances. We have uniforms out there now doing just that. Myself and Andy here are dealing with your family. I'll go next door to speak to Jacob after."

"Jacob. Right." Suzie took the mug Andy handed to her and left the kitchen, shuffling, head down.

Andy raised his eyebrows then brought Helena's tea over. He went back to the side to make Robbie a cuppa, and Robbie himself came in, closing the door behind him. His skin was grey, a vast difference to when they'd first arrived. Perhaps he'd been listening to what they'd been talking about.

"Take a seat." Helena gestured to the chair Suzie had vacated and gave him a smile in the hopes it would put him at ease.

Robbie had been at work at the times of both murders. Olivia had rung his boss and checked; Phil had accessed the company's CCTV. Robbie had been doing two shifts lately, six hours during the day, then going back for ten at night until two a.m. Helena supposed it was to help pay off the council tax bill Suzie had mentioned.

"How are you bearing up?" she asked.

Robbie sat and shrugged. "I'm poleaxed, to be honest. Their mum died recently, and now this. For Suzie to lose her parents *and* her two sisters…"

"Yes, this family has had a fair few tragedies, I have to say. Life can be cruel sometimes." She gave him the same warning she'd given Suzie, then told him about the sewing, flowers, varnish, shaver, and duck.

Robbie's face paled, white painting over the grey, and he looked like he might be sick. Andy handed him a coffee, and Robbie accepted it, seeming grateful to have something normal to do. He wrapped his hands around the mug and stared at Helena.

"I don't...I don't understand," he said.

"Nor do we. Has Suzie confided in you at all, about items like those I mentioned?"

"Why would she? Why would anyone know the reasons those things were put...there?"

"This is what we need to find out. It's significant, important to the killer. It means something. Suzie says she has no idea."

Robbie frowned. "Well, the only thing I can offer is all the girls hate flowers and nail varnish. I just thought it was a quirk, you know, sisters banding together to dislike the same thing. They're all a bit tomboyish, so I put it down to that. Then there was Emma with her not digging colours—I admit I find that bloody weird. Who hates colours, all of them?"

"Do you know why a pair of rose-patterned gardening gloves with false nails on them would be left at Callie's?"

"Pardon?" Robbie blinked, and his hands shook, sloshing some coffee over the rim of the mug. He flicked one hand to get rid of the spillage, then wiped his fingers on his jeans.

"Didn't Suzie tell you about that?" Helena asked.

"No!"

"I see." *Why didn't she?* "Do you know why a rubber duck would be left at Emma's?"

"No!" he said, drawing out the O. "That's just plain weird."

The man honestly seemed as perplexed as Helena. If she was any judge, he wasn't bullshitting. He had no idea at all. But all the women disliking flowers and polish... She wouldn't badger Suzie about it again today, but she'd be asking Jacob in a minute. Maybe he'd be more forthcoming.

"Okay, thank you for your time. I gather you've been told you have to stay here until this is all over, yes?" She stood.

Robbie got up, too. "Yes. What about the kids going to school?"

"I'll get Clive, the officer outside, to contact the head and sort out some work they can do from home. It's best neither you, Suzie, nor Jacob are seen. You're aware, what with two sisters being murdered, what that might imply?"

He nodded. "That Suzie could be next."

"Or Jacob, you... Your *children*."

"What?" His eyes bugged.

"Do you know of anyone who has a grudge against you?" she asked.

"Not that I'm aware of, but I'll have a think about it."

"You do that. Here's my card." She ferreted in her pocket and took one out, handing it to him.

He held it in both hands, turning it around repeatedly. "I...I don't know what to say or think."

"I can imagine it's dreadful."

"Suzie's going to go mad with the boys home all day. They're...a bit naughty."

"Then you'll have to get creative and keep them occupied, won't you. Better than being dead," she said.

He stared at her, the reality of what she'd said obviously sinking in. "God."

"Indeed. Let's hope He keeps you safe, eh?"

CHAPTER FOURTEEN

Suzie sat in the living room, staring into space. The boys were being good for once—maybe they'd picked up on the tension and had thought it best to behave. They'd managed a quarter of the jigsaw, a farmyard scene with chickens and whatnot, a horse or two in a paddock behind a three-bar fence.

Stratton was getting too close to the truth, and Suzie was crapping her damn self. She'd wanted to say something in the kitchen, the words had been right there on her tongue, but the thought of *him* finding out meant she'd kept the secret, same as she had all these years. But to find out her sisters had been sewn up and those...*things* had been placed inside them... He'd gone to a whole new level. He'd never been a nice person, she'd disliked him even before he'd started their sessions, but now? He was mad. Had to be.

If she kept her mouth shut, he wouldn't come for her.

But what if she said something out of turn and he came for her next?

A chill swept through her at the memory of the sessions. She thought back to her first encounter. God, she'd been so content that day, then he'd come along and ruined it.

Ruined everything.

Suzie had laughed so hard all day her tummy hurt. It had been such fun so far, what with it being Emma's birthday, and on a Saturday, too.

It was July, so that meant a beautiful, sunny day, temperatures soaring into the nineties. Emma's friends were just arriving, and Suzie stood on the bottom step of the stairs and watched the parade of guests walk by then go through into the back garden. Such pretty dresses, everyone dolled up in their finest, nice shoes over lacy ankle socks. Many a head had ponytails, so severely tight the kids' eyes looked squinty, and others had Alice bands holding curly locks off foreheads. Presents, clutched in small hands, had bright paper, so many different colours, and some even had glittery bows. Cards were Sellotaped to the sides or tops, and Suzie couldn't wait to see what Emma had got. They'd have to wait until after the party for that, though, when the family sat round the dinner table and squealed every time a new gift was revealed.

The front door closed at last – everyone had arrived – and Mum bustled off to follow the bunch of girls. Some neighbours had come round to help with the rabble, and adult voices filtered inside, chased by the chatter of several girls all talking at once.

Emma bounded in from outside to tug Suzie along, out into the glorious sunshine. Dad had set the boom box up, propping it on a stack of bricks he'd bought to build a nice wall around a fountain once he found the time to do it. Music blasted, all the girls squealing then singing along. Suzie watched the melee in fascination, happy the party was going exactly as they'd hoped it would.

Soon it was the feast, and everyone lined up at the trestle table by the fence, nice and orderly, considering how excited they were, and Mum passed out white paper plates as the girls selected what they wanted – ham, cheese, or beef paste sandwiches, sausage rolls, cheese sticks, cupcakes, Monster Munch, and all manner of lovely things, and best of all, red jelly right at the end in transparent plastic beakers. Dad said he'd put a dob of Neapolitan ice cream on the top once it came to pudding time, and maybe sprinkles if they were lucky.

Suzie tagged on the end of the line, and once all were seated in a circle on blankets covering the grass, munching away, Dad winked at her and switched the CD to the Spice Girls.

Emma almost wet herself – she had no idea he'd picked the music up in Tesco on his way home from work last night, Suzie and Callie sworn to secrecy so they didn't spoil the surprise. Strains of Two Become One wailed out of the speakers and various mouths between bites of food, some even singing with grub on show until Mum said that wasn't very nice, was it, and where's your manners?

After the food had gone, pass the parcel came next, everyone belting out a-zig-a-zig-ahhhh long after the music had been paused for someone to open a layer. The prize, won by Miranda Bellsthrop, a Barbie with a sparkling pink dress and high-heeled rubbery shoes, seemed the envy of everyone else, and more than a few groans went round – there were a couple of pouts in place, too.

Still, it didn't spoil anything for Suzie. Parties were wonderous things, and even the air seemed to be celebrating right along with them. Suzie reckoned it fizzled, just like the excitement in her belly, or that might be because she'd had a bit too much pop.

Hide and seek was proposed after the jelly and ice cream, and while everyone scampered off to find a place to hole up amid Mum calling out that no one was to go in her bedroom and mess up the piles of ironing on the bed – "I didn't spend all morning pressing that for it to get creased, you know!" – Suzie waited. She knew exactly where she was going to tuck herself away.

She crept indoors, smiling at the shrieks and pattering footsteps where the guests rushed to scurry *under beds or stand stock still behind doors. Emma had stayed in the garden, counting to one hundred with her hands over her eyes, her voice sailing through into the hallway, where Suzie stood in front of the door to the cupboard under the stairs.*

In she went, trampling on shoes, the smell of feet heady in the muggy air. She pinched her nose, closed the door, and wedged herself in the triangular end where there might be spiders, but it didn't matter, she wanted to win the prize.

Emma shouted, "Coming, ready or not!"

Suzie's stomach clenched, and she squeezed her eyes shut, as if that meant Emma wouldn't know she was in the cupboard. Footsteps thundered past, then a "Found you!", and Emma went off in search again, up the stairs this time.

Suzie opened her eyes.

The door peeled outwards, and she stared. Maybe someone was joining her in the hiding place. It was him, poking his head inside and spotting her. She didn't like him, never had, but if she kicked up a fuss, she'd spoil Emma's day, and that wasn't something Suzie was prepared to do.

He climbed in, closing the door behind him, and he was so big, and the cupboard seemed to shrink, and Suzie grew uneasy, trapped there with him.

"Go away," she said. "I got here first."

"And I got here second."

Then he told her things — things that frightened her — and asked, "So, are you going to keep the secret?"

She nodded, unable to do anything else, stuck as she was in the triangle. She wanted Mum or Dad, but he'd said they wouldn't believe her if she told them what he'd said, so she kept her mouth shut.

Then he touched her, and suddenly Suzie hated parties, hated music, hated buffet food, but most of all, she'd hated forget-me-nots and purple nail polish once he'd explained that they were indicators of their 'sessions'.

She'd keep quiet. He mustn't be allowed to kill anyone. She couldn't stand the guilt if he did.

CHAPTER FIFTEEN

Helena left Suzie's flat and smiled at Clive. "She's not letting on, is she," she whispered to Andy. Then to Clive, "Open this door for me, will you, please, so I can see what her brother has to offer."

Clive let her in, and Helena walked inside, the layout the same but a mirror image. Andy followed her and shut the door.

"Jacob?"

"In here," came his incredibly deep voice.

Helena glanced at Andy, and he raised his eyebrows as if to say: *Let's get this over with.* She nodded in answer then entered the living room.

Jacob sat on a sofa and, like next door, the room was bare of everything except the essentials. Soulless, uninviting, but it did the job for those who had to stay here. Empty crisp packets surrounded him, probably from the Waitrose delivery stash, and it appeared he'd chomped his way through half a twenty-four pack of Walkers. A box of Jaffa Cakes balanced on his vast lap, his rotund belly giving them a cuddle.

"How are you?" she asked.

Helena sat on a chair adjacent. Andy remained standing. The sofa was only a two-seater, and Jacob took up most of it — him and his junk food. A bottle of Diet Coke leant against him, as though it wanted to join the Jaffas in the love fest.

"Devastated," he said. "Who wouldn't be when their sisters... God, I can't even bring myself to say it."

"I understand. Sorry our interview has been delayed."

"Emma's fault," he said.

Helena forced herself not to frown. "Emma hardly meant for this to happen."

Jacob opened his mouth to speak then shut it again. Grief had a funny way of affecting some people. Maybe he was going through the angry stage, having possibly been through the tears yesterday over Callie, although his eyes gave no sign of it.

Something about him had been bugging her, so she may as well get it off her chest right away.

"Why did you opt to go to work when this had happened? Most people need time to take it all in."

"I'm not most people."

God, he's a surly bastard, isn't he?

Andy coughed — or was that a disguise for something he'd said? Wanker, probably.

"Okay. Where were you on the night Callie died?" Helena clasped her hands over her knees.

Jacob grunted. "At work. As well as doing deliveries, I sometimes stay behind to help the night staff stack shelves. I need the money." He gestured to the food. "I've got an addiction."

"And last night, when Emma died?"

"Same thing. Check with the manager. She'll tell you." He opened the Jaffa Cake box then pulled out a packet of twelve.

"I'm sure she will." She inwardly cursed at having not checked in with Olivia and Phil about Jacob's whereabouts. Then again, if he hadn't been at work, one of them would have rung her to say so. "Do you know of anyone who would have wanted to do this to Callie and Emma?"

"No idea. They're a pair of buggers, those two. Could have been into all sorts of things for all I know." He crammed a cake in his mouth.

"What do you mean by 'buggers'?"

"Always tarting it about, aren't they. They couldn't be like Suzie and settle down. It's like

141

they're on a destruction course where their main aim is to shag around."

He's talking about them as if they're still alive.

"So you're saying they were promiscuous?" she asked.

"Let's just say they've had a lot of fellas, one-night stands. They've never been in a proper relationship. I don't know why they'd want to have sex with every Tom, Dick, or Harry, but there you go. They do."

She'd have to see if Olivia had picked anything like that up from speaking to their friends. Callie's work colleagues at Waitrose hadn't revealed anything when they'd been spoken to, and Olivia would be going to The Villager's Inn, probably about now, to chat to all the staff. Those who always worked evenings had agreed to go to the pub and meet with her.

"Did either of them have any close friends?" Helena couldn't believe he'd finished all the cakes in the time she'd been thinking.

"They hang around with each other. Thick as thieves, the pair of them." He opened the Coke and glugged some down, straight from the bottle.

Helena's stomach churned. She hoped he wouldn't be sharing that drink with anyone else. "We were led to believe that Callie was a little —"

"Slapper?"

Good grief. "No. Perhaps paranoid. Do you know anything about that?"

He gave a hearty belch then screwed the lid on the Coke. "What, her keep saying a man was in her house?" He let out a raspy laugh. "Listen, she's been a bit weird ever since we had a night in the tent in our back garden. She changed after that. Got all jumpy, always glancing about as if someone was going to leap out at her. I reckon she had a nightmare in the tent. You know, from being outside and not safe in the house."

He stared into space, and Helena waited for more. Sometimes, people liked to gabble to fill the silence.

"Then when she got older," Jacob said, "and the rest of us moved out, she stayed with our mum, didn't want to leave her on her own. Then Mum died" — his lip wobbled — "and Callie had to live by herself. Emma didn't want her sharing her place. Said Callie put on too many colours. You know, loud clothes and shoes."

What a strange thing to have an issue with. The bleakness of Emma's house appeared in Helena's mind, and she shivered at how stark it all was.

"Ours was a council house, when we were kids, like, and the bastards wouldn't let Callie take on the tenancy because she didn't have any kids." He let out a growl. "It was a three-bed — they needed it for someone with a family. They offered her a crummy bedsit in a shared house, so she rented instead. The other people there probably wouldn't have liked her bringing man after man home, so it was a good job she didn't go there. Maybe if she'd taken it, she wouldn't be dead. On her own in her place, there wasn't anyone to save her."

Helena shook her head. That was a lot of information in one go. She glanced at Andy to make sure he'd jotted it down. He nodded, as if sensing her looking at him.

"So you don't know why she changed after the camping?"

"No bloody idea. I was just a kid myself. I didn't hang around with them, my sisters. I played with the lads of a family we knew. We had barbecues and holidays with them, stuff like that." He ripped open a bag of crisps and all but tipped them down his throat. Prawn cocktail.

She waited a while for him to chew then asked, "When did your food addiction start?"

"What the fuck's that got to do with you?" Crisps showered out of his mouth.

Tread carefully. "I'm asking in case it was around the same time Callie became jumpy as a child. Was it near when your dad died?"

He swallowed the food and nodded. "For me it was, but Callie was a long time before that."

"Okay. Please don't snap at me, I'm just trying to help, but would you like me to put you

144

in touch with someone about your addiction? It may get worse now you have new trauma to deal with. I'm worried you're going to do yourself some damage."

He stared at her, mouth open, remnants of soggy crisps on his tongue. "You'd do that for someone you don't know, would you? There's got to be a catch."

"No, there isn't. Do you want help? I know of a lady who runs a class. Maybe you could just go for one and see how you feel. It's a charity, so it wouldn't cost you anything. You go along and chat with people who have issues. Alcoholics, smokers, recovering drug addicts, and other people who have a similar thing to you."

He continued to stare.

"Have a think about it," she said, unlacing her cramping fingers. "Now, I must ask this… Your comments about your sisters were disparaging." *Downright horrible.* "Did you like them?"

"Like them? I *love* them! I just don't like what they get up to. It winds me up, makes me sound like I don't give a toss. They're better than that. Opening their legs all the time…it's not exactly good for them, is it? I want them to be happy, to be cared for properly. Losing our dad so young, I felt protective over them, and it doesn't stop even though we're older."

Bless him. "Do you know any of the men they slept with? I'll need to speak to them."

"I don't. I just know they do it. They talk about it with Suzie. She doesn't like what they get up to either."

She explained that she was going to tell him something upsetting, then went on to give him the news she'd given Suzie and Robbie. "Do those items mean anything to you?"

"Fucking hell... That's just... I can't imagine why anyone would want to do that." He rubbed his eyes with the heels of his hands, then lowered them to his lap. "Now there's a thing. I remember Dad's shaver going missing and him having a mare about it because it'd not long been a Christmas present from our mum. He never did find it. What the bloody hell would she have that inside her for?"

"We have no idea, Jacob. It's incredibly disturbing and upsetting. What about the flowers and the nail varnish?"

"No clue why they'd have been left there, but I remember those sorts of flowers being outside their room for a good few years. Once a week they were there, then later on, they appeared every night."

What the hell? Outside their bedroom? "Was there any explanation given for them being there?" How she managed to stay professional and not screech that question was anyone's guess.

He smiled sadly. "Yeah, Emma said it was to ward off a demon, something like that. Something bad or other anyway. She's into all that fantasy stuff. Loves her dragons and fairy tales. Castles, all that sort of thing. I just shrugged it off as her being her usual self."

The dragon tattoo on her foot…

"She has tatts of them—the dragons, I mean." His eyes misted. "One on her foot, another on her arm, a castle behind it. She was on about getting a big one to cover her back," he went on. "She won't be able to do that now…"

Ah, here it came… He cried then, big, choking sobs, and Helena got up to sit on the arm of the sofa and rest a hand on his shoulder. What an utter mess. She looked at Andy, who shuffled from foot to foot. He never had been much good at consoling the bereaved.

Once Jacob had calmed down, she crouched in front of him. "I know this is hard, but are you up for more questions?"

He nodded.

"What about the nail varnish?"

"All I know is that none of my sisters can stand it, which doesn't make sense because they put in on as kids." He shrugged and sniffed.

"Do you remember when the flowers first started appearing outside their door? It doesn't have to be exact, just a guess."

He looked at the ceiling, opening a bag of crisps. Salt and vinegar this time. "I must have been about eight, which meant Suzie was nine, Emma was seven, and Callie six. God bless our mum, she had a kid a year. I was playing on the landing when I noticed the purple flowers. I don't know what they were. Small things, lots of them on a stem. They had a yellow bit in the middle. Lilac, the petals were, maybe with a bit of blue. I had a red toy car, and I was making it drive along the carpet. I got it for my eighth birthday."

"Okay. So the flowers were there, and Emma said it was to do with a demon. What about the polish, though? Can you think of —"

"Purple for Suz, pink for Emma, and red for Callie. They only wore it for a day at a time, though, then they took it off. Picked at it, they did. Mum thought they'd been nicking hers, but Suz said her friend had given it to them. I remember that night. We were eating at the table, Mum saying they had to give the nail varnish back, and all the girls had a bloody meltdown, so Mum backed off." He frowned, as though the scene played out in his head.

Helena imagined a family meal, Mum, Dad, and their four children sitting around the table, talking about their day, the girls toying with their food after the upset, little hiccups every so often from their tears.

"Did they say which friend gave it to them?"

"No."

Did that friend have something to do with this?
"Did they say where they got the flowers from?
Were they real?"

"Plastic. And no, sorry, I didn't ask. I wasn't
that bothered. So long as I could play on the
landing, I didn't give a shit. Now the flowers
and the varnish are significant, I wish I..."

"You were little. No one was to know what
would happen in the future. Please don't blame
yourself."

"I'm their brother. I should have been able to
help them. I shouldn't have kept banging on
about what they got up to in bed. They probably
think I hate them, that I think they're disgusting.
Now I can't tell them I just wished they'd have
more respect for themselves because... Fuck's
sake." He reached out to lay a hand on a packet
of crisps.

The poor man needed food for comfort.

"Look, we're going to leave you for now, but
we'll see you tomorrow, just in case you think of
something overnight." Helena stood, her leg
muscles protesting. "It's fine to go and see Suzie
if you need to. Clive will let you in." She didn't
have the heart to tell him off now for the
Waitrose delivery. She understood why he'd
done it. "If you need any more shopping, let

Clive know, and he'll deal with it for you, okay?"

Jacob nodded.

With nothing more to say for now, Helena and Andy left the flat.

Helena quietly told Clive about the food addiction. "So if he needs more, sort it out for him. It might be the only thing keeping him together at the moment."

"All right, guv," Clive said.

"We need to go back to see Suzie," she said.

Clive let them in, and again, Helena called out.

Suzie poked her head out from the living room into the hallway. "Yes?"

"I need a quick word in the kitchen." Helena smiled and led the way.

Robbie was in there, making a drink, and he walked out to give them privacy. Suzie shut the door and stood by the sink.

"Suzie, your brother told us about the flowers outside your bedroom door in the family home. Can you tell me anything about that?"

"Oh, those. They were just some plastic things Callie liked."

"Callie?"

"Yes." Suzie laughed. It sounded false. "She liked to pretend we had an indoor garden."

"So it wasn't Emma wanting to ward off a demon?"

Suzie's face paled, and she blinked. "No! Did Jacob tell you that?"

"Yes." Helena stared, waiting for an explanation.

"He doesn't know what he's talking about. It was Callie and her garden obsession."

You slipped up there, madam. "So the gardening gloves left at her home perhaps has a reason after all, then, even though you claimed you had no idea why they'd be there."

Suzie's mouth opened and closed.

"An 'obsession' is pretty strong, don't you think?" Helena said. "It isn't something you're likely to forget, but it seems you did when I asked about the gloves."

Cheeks flushing bright red, Suzie stared at the floor.

"You know exactly what it's about, don't you?" Helena accused.

"No. I told you before, I have no idea."

"I'm going to find out in the end," Helena said. "With or without your help." She paused, waiting for a reaction.

When nothing came, she stormed out of the flat, Andy rushing to keep up.

"Speak to you tomorrow, Clive," she said.

"All right, guv. Someone's coming to take over here about six. Unfortunately, we can't spare anyone for keeping guard out the back because of the cuts."

"Righty oh." Helena checked through the glass in the block's main door for anyone hanging around, then she went outside. In the car, she thumped the steering wheel.

Andy got in. "She's hiding something."

"You're telling me." She snatched her phone out of her pocket and rang Olivia. "Anything for me?"

"Absolutely nothing from the pub except that Emma liked the men, as in—"

"I know. Anything else?"

"Afraid not. Drawing blanks all over the place."

Helena checked the time on the dash. "You and Phil go home. We'll start again in the morning. Thanks for your hard work today."

"Tarra," Olivia said.

Helena slid her phone away. "I'll take you home, save you getting the bus."

"Thanks."

They didn't speak on the journey. Helena was too pissed off. A lying family member didn't sit well with her. She dropped Andy off then went home, ready to sit and veg on the sofa all night. Then she remembered she had a date with Zach, and her mood brightened.

CHAPTER SIXTEEN

The date hadn't really been a date so far, and Helena asked herself if it was just a sexual attraction or whether they really could make a go of it. She fancied him, there was no denying that, but if all they were going to do was talk shop, she could do that with Andy. She wanted someone she could chat bullshit to, locking her work day out, but she hadn't had that with Marshall either. He'd seemed overly interested in what she did for a living, to the point she'd questioned why he wanted to know.

Now here she was with Zach, nagging about the same things. Since they'd sat at a corner table, they'd talked about the case, mainly Zach's findings in Emma's PM. She'd recently had her pubic hairs removed. Helena couldn't help but wonder if that was a link to the shaver, some hidden message she was supposed to figure out—or was it a message to Suzie? The blood being washed off while Emma rested on Zach's table revealed a bruise on her forehead and the dragon and castle tattoo Jacob had mentioned. How very sad to have so many dreams and imaginings about a fairy land only to have them and her life snuffed out so cruelly. Emma would never see them in her mind's eye again.

"Are you all right?" Zach leant over and rubbed her arm.

Him doing that had her wishing they weren't out in public. "Yes, just thinking about how wicked life is at times, that's all."

"The things we see…"

"I know."

"So how are you getting along with Andy now? Better?" He left his hand there.

She was glad it didn't send her screeching off on a tangent like it did to some women who'd been through what she had. Luckily, she'd been able to separate her traumatic experience from normal touches. "Oh, he's much better. We're still going to the gym first thing."

"You what? He didn't call it off?" His eyes widened.

Helena smiled and tried placing her hand on his to see how she felt about it. *Good.* "He wants to sort himself out. Fancies Louise, doesn't he, so he wants to be in with a chance."

"That's actually pretty sweet. Who'd have thought gruff, moany old Andy would have a soft side."

"He doesn't know how to show it, that's all. I haven't seen it in all the years we've worked as a pair, but I'm hoping it'll come out in the future. I don't think he'll ever give up the moaning, though, but he's trying."

"So… Where do *we* go from here?" he asked.

Bloody hell. She hadn't been expecting him to switch it round to them. "No idea. Play it by ear? Day to day?"

"Exactly what I thought. No rushing."

"I'm glad. We've both jumped from our last relationships into another, and…"

"Yep, I can imagine you need space after…you know."

Uthway and Marshall.

They continued talking, thankfully not about them or work, and by ten o'clock, Helena had to admit she needed to get home. Tiredness was a killer. He walked her back, pushing his bike alongside him.

"You can still get arrested for being pissed up on a bicycle you know," she said.

"I only had two pints—and I sipped them."

She could have waxed lyrical about still being over the limit, that reactions would be impaired, but really, she couldn't be arsed. "I'll let you off. On this occasion." She didn't add that maybe if he stayed the night next time, he could drive over in his car instead.

Baby steps, not a ruddy great giant's.

Outside her front door, he kissed her — nothing manic, just nice and tender. It was strange after being used to Marshall's bruising efforts and —

Don't think about that.

With her body tingling, she said goodnight and went inside, forcing herself not to turn around and ask him in. She closed the door after he'd ridden away and pressed her back to it, smiling.

A loud knock startled her, and she swung the door open, laughing, expecting to see a bruised and scraped Zach where he'd gone over the handlebars and landed in the road.

Marshall stood there.

Shit.

"Oh, go away," she said, swinging the door forward.

He stuck his hand out and stopped it shutting. "Who's that?"

Whatever she'd seen in this man was long gone, buried, covered over with lumps of hate and the loss of respect. His narrowed eyes reminded her of a spiteful animal, and his flared nostrils meant he was gearing up to have one of the rages he was so good at flying into.

"If you don't leave, I'll call the police. You're harassing me." She dealt with pricks like this at work, but somehow, with it being personal, she couldn't find the mantle she usually used — the one that lent her courage and had her voice sounding abrupt.

"Harassing, my arse." He sneered.

God, he was so ugly inside. A bitter, selfish man.

"Who is it?" he demanded.

Maybe if she told him, he'd bugger off. "A bloke from work."

"Oh, so you kiss all men from work, do you?"

"That's no longer any of your business."

"Been having it away with that Andy as well, have you? I bet you get up to all sorts, you fucking slag."

He'd gone too far now. Her professional head screwed itself on, and she took her phone out of her pocket and held it up. "Really, Marshall? You want to do this?"

His face reddened. "Just you watch yourself, that's all I'm saying."

"You've just threatened a police officer."

"Oh, piss off, you stupid bint."

He swaggered down the path and out onto the pavement, going in the opposite direction to Zach. Helena closed the door and put the chain and bolts across. She'd be sorting out the restraining order tomorrow, no dicking about now. He needed to learn what 'we're over' meant.

Chilled from not only the winter air but the confrontation, she kicked her shoes off then went into the kitchen. She made a hot chocolate and took it up to bed, placing it on her chest of drawers. Needing a shower, feeling filthy just for having been near Marshall, she jumped under the spray, cursing him for ruining the memory of her first kiss with Zach. Whenever she looked back on Zach's gentleness it would be swiftly followed by Marshall's appearance and the wanky things he'd said.

In her pyjamas, she got in bed and sipped her drink, finally warming up. Her mind drifted to Uthway, as it usually did just before sleep. Where was he? What was he doing? Would he ever make good on his promise and come for her?

She shivered and set her cup on the bedside cabinet, then closed her eyes, the lids pink on the insides from the glow of her lamp. She didn't sleep without it on. Not anymore. Not since what had happened with Uthway.

Sleep came calling, ushering her into its world of trickery, the ruler of the dark hours with the power to either give her sweet dreams or horrendous nightmares. It held all the cards, and she could only hope, as Uthway's face morphed into Marshall's, that tonight she'd be left in peace.

"Shut your mouth, you fucking bitch."

It was pitch-black, and Helena couldn't see or tell who'd spoken. Was it Uthway or that other bloke who'd brought her here? They sounded the same, the menacing nuances floating to her even after the words had died out.

She huddled into the corner she'd been thrown in, shivering, grit digging into her bare backside. Her clothes…she needed her clothes. Some dignity, even though it was dark and he couldn't see her.

Why had he told her to shut her mouth? She must have whimpered. She couldn't remember; everything was a blur. Minutes all meshed into one another, stretching into hours, days, or so she assumed. It was bloody freezing, so maybe her teeth had chattered, and that was why he'd barked at her.

"You need sorting once and for all, you do," he said.

She could imagine what he meant. Killing her. Getting her out of his way for good. She tried to bring forth her training, what to do in a situation like this, but it wouldn't come. It remained elusive, hovering just out of reach, teasing, whispering that she was on her own, and let's just see how you get yourself out of this one, you silly little cow. And she had been a silly

159

cow. She'd gone against protocol, as usual, and thought she could tackle Uthway by herself.

Wrong. So wrong.

"But I have another use for you."

She didn't dare answer him.

She sensed him come closer, although his footsteps were so faint she could be hearing things that weren't even there. But the air around her was different, charged now with the buzz of electricity or whatever the hell it was when people were near each other. The hairs on her arms stood on end, and she clamped her teeth to stop herself from crying out. She didn't need another beating. The last one had left her drained and aching. Instead of concentrating on him being near, she imagined what she looked like now. Filthy. Skin with a slight sheen from sweat. Hair stringy, hanging in lank strips. Bruised. Nose broken. Blood from that nose crusting on her face, her chest, where it had dripped.

"If anyone comes here to rescue you," he said, "and finds me, I'll kill you before they can even step foot inside the door, you got that?"

It was Uthway. She could tell from his body odour and rancid breath — coffee laced with a whiskey so strong her eyes watered. She closed them — like that was going to block him out — and wished she didn't see him in her damn head so much. Tracking him for months, so many hours of surveillance, meant she knew every single crevice on his face, every pore, every fleck of lighter blue in his navy irises.

And she hated him. For what he'd done and what he was doing now.

"Answer me," he breathed.

Her stomach contracted. "No one's coming. I didn't tell them where I was going."

"So you say." The air carrying his words was hot and settled on her cheek.

"If you think about how long I've been here, it should tell you no one's coming," she said and waited for a slap for having spoken without being asked a question or having permission to say anything.

"Six hours is nothing," he snapped.

Six hours? Was that all? Fuck, it felt like six days.

"They'll be waiting for it to get dark, I'll bet," he said.

Then he licked her ear, and it was a wonder she didn't shriek or shy away from him. He'd already told her, after he'd raped her earlier, that to act as though she didn't like him near her would be a 'black mark' in her book. She needed to learn to like it.

"Then they'll come out with their guns and Tasers," he went on. "They'll burst in here to get you, only you'll be dead."

She'd asked him where she was when she'd first been thrust in here, and he'd told her to shut her gob if she knew what was good for her. Blindfolded, she'd had to rely on her ears, and the shush and whoosh of the sea had told her she was somewhere close to shore. It was too loud to be anywhere else.

His friend had brought her here in a car after abducting her from a surveillance spot where she'd been taking photos of Uthway and his men shepherding kidnapped women into a run-down house on the outskirts of Smaltern. Maybe sunlight had glinted off her binoculars, she didn't know, but the man had come up behind her, slapped a hand over her mouth, and dragged her backwards. She'd fought, of course she had, but he was a beast of a creature, well over six feet with a muscular build and the strength of two.

"What have you got to say about that?" he asked.

Say about what? She'd forgotten what he'd been talking about.

"I don't know," she said.

"What, you don't know what to say about me killing you?"

"No."

"Scared, are you?"

She wouldn't give him the satisfaction of knowing. "I don't care anymore." And it was strange, but she didn't. How could only six hours of mental torture and the violation of her body reduce her to a shell so quickly? Tired from whatever the hell they'd injected her with, she had no strength to fight. To speak.

It scared the shit out of her, and a burst of adrenaline flashed through her. Fight or flight. Live or die. About to tell him to go and fuck himself, she stopped. A creak rang out, grating on her nerves, then a long, slender sliver of light that seemed far away widened into a slice of the world outside her prison. With the adrenaline had come a clarity of sorts, and she made out the time of day – it was still *light – the interior of her surroundings – possibly a large metal storage container – and the silhouette of another man.*

"You're meant to give the proper knock, dickhead," Uthway said.

"Sorry, boss. Didn't realise you were in here."

"Yeah, well..." Uthway sniffed. "Close the fucking door then!"

The darkness came back, and footsteps echoed. Something was wrenched down over her head, material, and it tickled her shoulders. A bag of some sort. If her hands weren't tied behind her back, she'd have ripped it off. Then a light came on, and she strained to see through the black weave, tiny specks of brightness filling her vision.

"Any good, was she?" the newcomer asked.

"They're always good when they fight it," Uthway said. "Find out for yourself, if you like. I need some grub."

Helena swallowed the lump in her throat. No, not that. Not again.

The creak shouted out again, then a clang when the door shut.

"All right then, Little Miss Pretty," the man said. "Spread 'em."

Helena shot up in bed, her heart thumping, her body drenched in sweat.

"I'm in my room, I'm in my room, I'm in my room…"

She rubbed her arms and breathed deeply. Shuddered. Shook her head to try to dislodge the remnants of the nightmare that insisted on lingering. The smell of Uthway and that man clung to the insides of her nostrils, and she reached out to grab her deodorant, spraying it in the air then inhaling so their stench was wiped out.

"I can't keep going like this."

Marshall had got annoyed whenever she'd had a bad dream, saying she disturbed his sleep with her mumblings and shrieks, and couldn't she be a bit more considerate? She'd stopped him staying over after that. Had stopped caring about him somewhere around that time, too. He had traits of Uthway and the unnamed man, and she couldn't bear it.

She glanced at the clock. Fuck. She hadn't set her alarm in time to go to the gym. Slinging on her training stuff, she then packed her work clothes and shoes in a small holdall and texted Andy to remember to do the same. She also apologised for being late. She'd shower at the gym, then they'd head straight to work after having a bite to eat at the leisure centre restaurant.

Outside Andy's, she went to toot the horn then remembered the early hour. He got in the car, bleary-eyed, his hair a mess, new gym clothes on along with white trainers, God bless him.

"I'll be on time in future," she said, driving off.

"I didn't mind. I got a few more minutes of shut-eye. This is going to kill me, you know that, don't you."

"No, it won't." She laughed. "Believe it or not, it'll give you more energy."

"How the hell do you work that one out?"

"Google is your friend."

She glanced in the rearview. A red car was right up her arse. She went a bit faster; so did they. She slowed; same for them.

"We've got a tail," she said.

Andy peered in the wing mirror. "I see it." He recited the number plate over and over while getting his phone out to access the note app, then plugged it in. "I'll ring the station."

"Wait for a bit, see if they follow us in here." She turned into the leisure centre car park and pulled up in one of the spaces closest to the building.

"They're over there," Andy said.

"I saw."

They got out, Helena ready to go over there if need be and ask what was going on, but the occupant of the car stepped out.

"Fucking Marshall," she said.

"Want me to say anything?"

"No, he uses this gym. That'll be his excuse for being here." She told Andy what had happened last night. "So he clearly thinks I'm shagging you and Zach."

Andy held up his phone and took a picture of Marshall. "This'll help matters. If he keeps this up, I'll have a fair few images we can use against him."

"Thanks," she said, locking the car. "Come on, let's get this over with."

They headed towards the glass double doors, and Helena glanced over her shoulder.

Marshall swiped a finger across his neck then pointed at her.

Helena pushed inside, determined not to let him get to her. She'd experienced scarier men than him in that storage container, so if he thought he could compete with their brutality and mental cruelty, he had another think coming, the twat.

CHAPTER SEVENTEEN

He stood outside the back of the flats where Suzie and Jacob had been taken, the early morning nip in the air chomping at his cheeks. His gloves kept his fingers warm, though. He couldn't be doing with them getting stiff. Not with what he had in mind. As with Callie, he had his trench coat and hat on. A sense of importance filled him whenever he slid his arms into the sleeves and covered his hair with the fedora. He was that foster bloke from years back then, Mr Jeffs, or like him anyway, important, someone who had the ability to make or break a life.

He'd been obsessed with Mr Jeffs' outfit from the moment he'd first seen it. He didn't wear it often, it was too distinctive, and his girlfriend —

well, his ex now, he supposed — had roared with laughter when he'd turned up in it, asking him if he thought he lived in the nineteen-twenties.

He hadn't liked that. He'd got mean with her, stroppy, and she'd stared at him oddly, as though she'd finally seen what he'd successfully hidden inside while with her. The darkness. The skill to hurt and maim and hate and…

Murder.

The system hadn't treated him kindly in his first thirteen years. He'd been shoved from pillar to post, looked after — or slung up, not brought up — by a series of 'parents' who didn't deserve that title. He'd acted out, understandably so, according to his young case worker, Mrs Featherstone, and when he'd been shipped to the Walkers, he'd found his forever home. He'd been touched too many times to count and hit until bruises covered him before then, and Mr and Mrs Walker had been the perfect parents.

The resentment towards their kids had festered, though, turning him sour.

Stop going back to the past. The future is what matters.

He tapped on the bedroom window, just a slight series of raps, knowing she'd wake. She was a light sleeper, and *he'd* made that so. He'd changed her and her sisters' sleeping patterns from the time he'd moved in to the time he'd moved out and beyond. The Walker girls had been his project, him punishing them for having a proper family when he'd never had one. Jacob—now he was a tosser, a fat little prick who hadn't liked sharing his bedroom with him for the years he'd been with the family. Jacob would get what was coming to him and all. Just by not having his parents and sisters, he'd know what it felt like to have no one to call your own.

To make that a complete task, he'd have to kill the bratty twins, but he had to draw the line at some point. Kids were off-limits when it came to death. But for other things…never.

I said, stop thinking about it.

He tapped the window again.

"Wake up, you little bitch," he whispered. "I'm here for you."

Suzie jolted awake for about the tenth time. It had been a shit night's sleep so far, and she was about to lose her temper. The flat was so quiet compared to their place, where the main road behind it had traffic even in the dark hours.

Something knocked.

She sat up and stared around the unfamiliar room, then at Robbie beside her. He was snoring, so she got up and went to check on the boys. They were splayed out, eyes closed, mouths wide open, catching flies as Dad used to say.

Then she had a look in the living room — nothing there or in the bathroom. Kitchen? She padded in, glancing around in the gloom. With the flat being so bare, there was nowhere for anyone to hide and not much furniture to imagine as someone hiding in the shadows.

So she flicked on the light.

And saw *him*.

He was at the back door, staring through the glass, that fucking awful hat on and his creepy mac. She stared, eyes going wide, and reached out to grip the worktop to steady herself, slapping her free hand over her mouth.

How had he found her?

What did he want?

A policeman was on the other side of the front door, sitting on a chair, keeping an eye out. If she just went to him and told him, *he'd* be caught, and all this would be over.

He shook his head, though, as if he'd poked around inside hers and knew what she'd thought. Then he opened his mouth and breathed on the glass, creating a cloudy patch. In it, he wrote: COME HERE.

Conditioned, frightened, she walked towards the door, and he twirled his finger as if to tell her to unlock it. She couldn't. Her boys were here —

he mustn't be allowed to get to them. His forehead bunched.

He breathed on the glass again, a wider patch, and wrote: JUST TO TALK.

Part of her believed him. After all, at times, he'd chatted to her fine when he'd dropped round for a cuppa. But the other half screamed: *No, don't do this!*

Suzie didn't know which one to listen to.

He rolled his eyes as though he thought her a bit daft, then waved and walked off, shrugging, past the kitchen window, towards Jacob's flat. No, he couldn't take her brother, too. Not poor Jacob, who struggled to cope with life in general, and God only knew how he was managing with Callie and Emma gone. *He* wasn't allowed to kill him, that hadn't been in the agreement. Jacob had never featured in all this.

Gathering her courage, she steeled herself to go out there and confront her tormenter. This had to stop, and if it meant *she* was the one doing the killing this time, then that was how it would be. If it kept her boys, Jacob, and Robbie safe, it was better that *he* was dead and she was in prison, wasn't it?

She quietly opened the drawer and took out a knife—it was one for bread, but it would have to do; there weren't any sharp, pointy ones. At the back door, she turned the key slowly, a millimetre at a time, so it wouldn't make a noise and wake Robbie or alert *him* as to what she was doing. She could creep up on him and…

"Do this. Just get on with it," she muttered, scared to death but at the same time so angry she couldn't think straight.

There was another knock, fainter. Was he tapping on Jacob's window?

"No, you're not playing your sick games with him."

Suzie opened the door and stepped outside, the path freezing and gritty on the soles of her feet. Her cotton pyjamas weren't thick enough to keep the chill out, and she was quickly cold. She glanced to the right, and there he was, his back to her, leaning his shoulder on the outer wall of the flats between Jacob's kitchen window and the door. Locking her family inside, she lowered the key to the ground then straightened up, holding the knife out in front of her. She walked forward, attention trained on his silhouette. Heart racing, she lunged, sweeping her arm across to slice the back of his head, but she wasn't quick enough, and he was facing her now, gripping her wrists so tight her fingers went limp. The knife dropped, landing on the path with a clatter.

"You should have done as I asked, *when* I asked, Suzie," he whispered.

With his hat brim pulled low, she couldn't see those hateful eyes of his, but they'd be darkening with his fury—going as dark as his blackened, demon-infested soul.

He shoved her against the wall of the flats, her cheek pressed to it, pain shooting down the side of her face, nodules of brick scraping her skin. Then he yanked her arms behind her and wrapped one of his large hands around her wrists. She vaguely registered she hadn't screamed, hadn't cried out for help, but hadn't that always been the way? Hadn't she always been silent and let him do whatever he wanted?

She fought the years of grooming, fought complying, fought that strange spell he'd had over her since she'd been a little girl, but it was as though she'd been transported back to being small again, and this big, mean hulk of a boy from the care system had infiltrated her and her sisters' minds and bodies as though he had the right.

Angry again, she struggled to throw him off, but she was out of shape and wheezing, her lungs constricting through fear and her inability to pull in a proper breath.

"Don't fight it," he whispered. "You knew it would come to this."

"But…but…" she gasped out. "I didn't…say a word. I…didn't…tell."

"I know."

"Then…" Oh God, she was going to have an attack. It was coming at her, chest seeming a rock-hard boulder, heavy without air. "Why are you here if I didn't…didn't tell the secret?"

"I lied."

His low chuckle terrified her, the same as it always did, and she wished she'd taken the initiative and moved them all away from here after she'd spoken to Emma about it. They should have packed a bag each and gone somewhere safe, then told the police. Instead, Emma was dead, and it looked like Suzie would be next. Then Jacob? Her boys? Robbie?

Oh God, no, please, not my boys…

"This is all Jacob's fault," he said, voice barely there.

What? She didn't understand. Jacob didn't know about any of this, did he?

"Please… I can't…breathe," she said.

"I don't know why you're worried about that. It'll all be over soon."

He pushed his body into her back, and his…oh, fucking hell, he was getting off on this. He had an…

She shuddered with revulsion.

If she wasn't panting, she might be able to scream, but she couldn't take in enough air to give her what she needed to make the noise. A cold spear went through her, but it didn't hurt, it just sucked the miniscule remains of breath from her lungs. Then another spear, seeming to go in reverse. Pain came then, shocking in its intensity, and he stepped back, letting go of her wrists. She stagger-turned to face him, and even in the darkness his smile was visible — wide and wicked, the leer he always gave when he got what he wanted.

She dipped her head, and a black stain spread on her pyjama top. If it wasn't sevenish on a winter morning, but summer, with a modicum of light, that stain would be red.

He held a knife up — not the bread one, but another, long and thin — and waved it in front of her face. "That's it, Suzie. Job done. Now Jacob will know what it's like to be me. He should have been happier about me sharing his room. Like I said, this is all his fault."

Suzie frowned, but it only camped out on her forehead for a second, her muscles going slack right along with her legs. She sank to the path and absurdly wondered if the brick behind her had a blood smear on it, showing her journey south. Her head felt as though it would burst — she needed oxygen, but her body wasn't in any state to help her out there.

She looked up at him, seeing the spiteful bastard for what he was — a maniac who'd been ruined in care and had been too broken for Mum and Dad to fix him. The damage had already been done before he'd tromped into their lives, and although he'd maintained an outer shell of being on the road to recovery, Suzie and her sisters had known better.

She closed her eyes and imagined kissing her boys for the last time. One more kiss before she had to leave them behind. One more brush of her lips against their soft cheeks. She wasn't going to make it, wasn't going to get out of this, she knew that. Then she kissed Robbie, thanking him for taking her away from the monster, the demon, and keeping her safe up until now. And Jacob, her dear brother, who would have no family left. She could only hope Robbie would look after him, get him help for his addiction.

So this is how it ends.

He slashed her throat.

CHAPTER EIGHTEEN

In her office, Helena sat in her chair and winced at her slightly aching muscles. She hadn't been to the gym for a while because of wanting to avoid Marshall—there was only one in town, so she'd seen him anyway—and now she was paying for it.

She should have known it wouldn't work out between them. Her life experiences in the force meant she had a more mature outlook on life compared to him. Come to think of it, she didn't know much about him really, just a few anecdotes from his past that didn't add up to anything she could patch together to glean what his life had been like before he'd met her. He'd talked at length about his girlfriends he'd been with prior to her, which was a bit strange to go into so much detail when you were with a new bird, but no names had been mentioned. He was a closed book, and she should never have started anything with him. But he'd won her over with his charming approach in The Blue Pigeon one night when she'd gone in for a swift voddy at the end of a particularly gruelling day.

They'd talked for a good couple of hours, and one vodka had turned to four, and going home alone had turned into him joining her, sharing her bed, her toothbrush in the morning — which had given her the shivers but she'd shrugged it off — and they'd met up often after that.

Now she thought about it, they hadn't actually said out loud they were a couple. They'd just drifted together, one date or meeting flowing into the next until the night he'd first got pissy with her and she'd asked herself what the hell she'd seen in him.

The aftereffects of finishing with him had turned nasty. Him doing what he'd done outside the leisure centre earlier had all but told her he wasn't going to let her go so easily. When she'd arrived at work, she'd gone through the rigmarole of sorting a restraining order. Louise had dealt with it, thankfully, and promised to look into him at some point today to see if anything weird came up.

Helena should have done that herself before she'd agreed to keep seeing him, but there hadn't seemed any need at first—and she'd wanted to be a normal person instead of relying on the database to check him out. Still, the wheels were in motion now, and once he was served with the order, he might back off. Mind, she knew more than anyone that restraining orders were a waste of time. Unless he actually harmed her, there wasn't much that could be done. He basically had carte blanche to follow her around all he liked and get away with it. That should change. The amount of women she'd dealt with who'd had an order out on someone and they'd ended up being beaten by their exes…

Bastards. Who did they think they were?

She was sifting through the paperwork from the past two days, reading what she'd written regarding Callie and Emma. It seemed so bizarre, what had happened, and with it down in black and white, it was like a bloody film plot. Someone out there had an agenda, and she needed to find them before anyone else got killed.

It wasn't looking likely at the moment.

Her desk phone rang, and she picked it up. "Yep."

"It's me, Louise."

"Oh, that was quick. Did you find anything on him?"

"I haven't had a chance to nose — a few people were brought in for booking. A call just came in. Suzie Walker has gone missing. Clive started his shift and went into the flats to check if everyone was all right, and it woke Robbie and the kids. They'd obviously slept in. So Clive asked where Suzie was, and Robbie called out to her…"

"Shit a brick. That isn't good. What about Jacob?"

"He's fine. Clive sent Robbie and the children into his flat for now because theirs is being treated as a crime scene."

"Why?"

"Um, out the back, in the communal garden, there's a knife and blood."

"Oh no…" Helena's heart sank. There had been no copper in the garden keeping watch. *Shit.* "That poor woman. I *knew* this was going to happen. How the fuck did they get found? Clive took their phones away, so they couldn't have contacted anyone."

"I don't know, guv. There are a couple of uniforms on the way there."

"Right, ring Clive for me and tell him not to touch anything, same for the uniforms. Have you arranged for SOCO?"

"No, thought I'd ring you first."

"Okay, do that now, and I'll go down there with Andy. Also send officers round to Suzie's actual address. We need to establish if anyone has been there. I'll speak to you soon."

She rushed out of her office and into the incident room. Olivia and Phil had their heads bent, concentrating on their computer monitors. Olivia had a list of something or other on hers, and Phil was scrutinising CCTV, probably for about the third or fourth time.

"Guys, Suzie Walker is missing. There's blood at the scene, so I'm imagining the worst."

"Blimey," Olivia said.

"Where's Andy?" Helena asked.

"In the loo," Phil said.

"What are you up to, Ol?" Helena stared at Olivia's back.

Olivia turned in her chair. "I've been looking at the past, digging a bit into the Walker family as a whole. I'm just on the schooling part at the moment. Might be an idea to collect all the names of kids in their classes and see where they are now — see if they match to the friends on their social media accounts. If any live around here still, they might remember spats the kids got into, someone with a bloody long grudge. It's all I can think of to do now. We've had dead ends so far on everything."

"Good thinking," Helena said. "Phil, I want you to get hold of the CCTV in the area of the flats, if there is any. Also check the camera feed from outside the building — we need to see what went on there. Suzie can't have left via the front door because a copper was out there. I'm going now, so get hold of me if you find anything, either of you."

"Got it, guv," Phil said.

Olivia smiled then faced her screen again.

Helena left the room and marched down the corridor. She tapped on the loo door. "Andy?"

"Yep…"

"Are you going to be long? Suzie's gone missing."

"Oh. Jesus. Um…"

"What's wrong?"

Andy coughed. "I'm…err…having trouble getting off the loo."

"Pardon me?"

"My legs. They've seized up on me."

She laughed, and it felt good and wicked at the same time. "You think this is bad. Wait until tomorrow, matey."

"Don't say that…"

"Grit your teeth and stand. We have to go. Get a move on." She leant against the wall and browsed Facebook. She had a Messenger alert so switched apps and had a look. One of her old colleagues who'd left Smaltern for Sunderland had sent a joke—a dark one about death—and she couldn't bring herself to giggle about it. Not today. She slid her phone away, and the sudden sound of the hand dryer had her jumping.

Andy ambled out of the loo on stiff legs, a frown in place.

"Oh, you poor thing," she said. "Those stairs are going to hurt. Come on."

She drove to the flats, and Helena had to park up the road a bit. A police car and a SOCO van hogged the spaces directly outside. Helena covered her hand with her sleeve and pushed the door open, then stepped into the foyer. Clive came up to her.

"What on earth happened?" she asked, taking blue booties and a pair of gloves out of a cardboard box beside the door.

Clive's expression was grim. "If I'd have been here…" He shook his head. "When I arrived, Kelvin said nothing was amiss, so I just let him go home. I went in to check on everyone…"

Helena popped the booties on. "Louise told me. So what the fuck happened out the back?" She snapped the gloves in place.

"Come and have a look." Clive opened the flat door. "By the way, two uniforms are off talking to the neighbours. There are six flats in this block, then they'll go out in the street and knock at the houses."

"Great, thanks."

Andy said, "Ouch!" under his breath a couple of times while bending down to sort his booties.

Helena nudged him in the ribs as Clive went into the flat. "Stop griping, man."

They went inside.

In the kitchen, Helena said, "That utensil drawer is open. Is there a list of what's in these places?"

"No idea," Clive said. "I'll make a call in a bit and check, but I think you'll find it's a knife."

"Shit."

She followed him outside, Andy waddling beside her pulling on his gloves, and Clive pointed to the knife. It was on the path, the blade and black handle clean as far as she could tell, the type used for bread with a serrated edge. A pool of blood was nearby on the path. She glanced up, and the blood on the wall had her closing her eyes for a brief moment.

"SOCO have already taken a swab of that and bagged Suzie's toothbrush for DNA testing," Clive said. "Probably safe to say it's hers, considering what happened to her sisters."

Helena's heart actually hurt. This was so sodding awful. "Christ. That blood on the path...there's so much. I'd say she, or whoever, was stabbed repeatedly."

Could Suzie have shanked the person who had killed her sisters, then run off, frightened about what she'd done? Helena wouldn't blame her if she had.

"The blood trail leads to the grass, as you can see," Clive said.

Helena stared at it. SOCO were on hands and knees, clearly hoping to find more blood so they could see where it went. She studied the garden. Just grass surrounded by a fence, although a couple of slats to the right were broken, and another four completely missing.

"Did you check over there?" she asked.

"Not yet," Clive said. "It all went a bit Pete Tong once I realised she'd gone AWOL."

She guessed he meant ringing it in and making sure Robbie and the lads went in with Jacob. "Okay, then that's the next job."

She picked her way over the grass, doing her best to skirt the direct line from the path to the fence. "This'll sting your leg muscles when you climb through," she said to Andy.

"I'm looking forward to it." The sarcasm was dripping.

She smiled and stepped over a low horizontal beam the fence slats were nailed to.

On the other side was a copse of sorts, with a bare strip made on the ground where people had obviously taken shortcuts to get through to the garden. Trees minus their leaves stood either side, their branches stretching overhead to create an arthritic-fingered canopy.

"Christ alive," Andy said, staggering through the hole in the fence.

"Oh, be quiet, you baby."

Helena peered between the array of slender tree trunks to the left. Nothing. She turned her head at the same time that Andy said, "Fuck me…"

"What?" she said.

"Through there, look."

She faced ahead. A path snaked into the distance, slicing a field in half. Because of the trees surrounding her, only a foot was in view, the heel resting on the path, the rest of her hidden behind the shield of branches. Helena moved forward, to the edge of the tree line, and there was Suzie to the right, flat on her back. A picnic blanket was beneath her, red-and-green tartan, and a pink plastic bowl with strawberries in it sat to one side.

What the bloody hell?

The cowhide print on her pyjama bottoms had Helena wanting to cry. A large bloodstain covered what she thought was a smiling cow's face on the cami top, although she couldn't be sure. Her mouth had been sewn up with purple thread, and Helena didn't need to guess where else it had been used.

What will be inside her?

"Oh, Suzie…" She wanted to tell the dead woman that if she'd just opened up and spoken to her, she'd still be alive now.

"Oh, bugger me," Andy said, coming to stand beside Helena. "Her neck... I'll um...I'll ring for Zach."

"Ask for more SOCOs," she said.

Andy walked down the path, taking his phone out, keeping his back to the body.

Helena's eyes stung. To stop herself from getting emotional, she scouted the area. The land on the left led to the cliff edge, so CCTV wasn't something they could check here. The faint sound of an angry sea shushed, and she imagined the killer dragging Suzie through the fence, dumping her, then bolting along the path, entering town from the outskirts somewhere in the distance.

She swung her attention back to Suzie. "Who did this to you, love?"

Andy called, "Zach's on his way."

Helena nodded. It seemed years ago she'd gone out for a drink with him. "We may as well go back through and speak to Robbie. Jacob, too. God, those poor little lads without their mother now."

Andy sighed. "I'd say watch how we go through the fence, but I didn't see any blood on it, did you?"

"No. Still, it might be microscopic, so best to be careful anyway."

She entered the tree area, mindful now of where she was walking. In the garden, she caught sight of Tom right over the other side. He was crouching, staring at the path.

"Tom?" she called.

He turned his head and lowered his face mask. "Morning."

"She's that way," she said, pointing to the broken slats. "Can you get a couple of others to go out there? She shouldn't be left alone. Someone might come along walking their bloody dog."

Tom got up and strode to her, and she stepped onto the path. Beside her, a blind covered a window and a curtain had been drawn across a door.

"Do you know whether there's easier access to those fields?" she asked. "It's going to be tough getting a tent and whatever through the fence gap."

Tom peered over there. "We'll just have to take more slats off. I'll get that sorted in a second."

"Okay. We're going in to talk to the brother and the husband, so can you direct Zach where to go once he gets here?"

"Will do." Tom walked off and tapped a colleague on the shoulder.

They both climbed through the fence.

Helena made eye contact with Andy, who was pale as anything.

"This is fucking shit," he said.

"I know." Helena grimaced. "And we've got to clean it up."

CHAPTER NINETEEN

Outside Jacob's flat, Helena and Andy took off their gloves and booties. She didn't want them knowing it was this serious until they'd answered a few questions.

Clive unlocked the door and whispered, "Dave Lund is in there with them. I thought it best they had a FLO as soon as possible. Plus, I wanted to make sure they didn't look out of the windows at the back and see anything."

"Thanks," Helena said.

She entered, Andy behind her. After the door closed, she looked down the hallway, and Dave popped his head out of the living room.

"Guv," he said.

She beckoned him with a curled finger. He walked up to her and lowered his eyebrows.

191

"We've found her," she whispered.

"Alive?" Dave asked.

Helena shook her head.

"God…" Dave blew out a long breath.

"How are they?" she asked quietly, shifting her eyes in the direction of the living room.

"Panicked at first, now they've gone quiet." He kept his voice low.

Helena had to lean in to hear him properly. "Panicked — in what way?"

"Jacob's been doing a lot of shouting, which hasn't helped keep the kids calm. Robbie's just standing there staring out of the window."

"What about the boys?"

"They're at the table colouring in. They seem a bit spaced out now, to be honest." Dave rubbed his forehead. "It's going to be a tough one, helping them through this."

"It's what you do best, though," she said and patted his arm. "I'm going to need to speak to them individually, so I'll use one of the bedrooms. I don't want them having an excuse to open the curtains and look out of the kitchen window."

Dave nodded, and she trailed him down the hallway into the living room.

Jacob was eating a chocolate cheesecake straight from the foil tray. Robbie gazed out into the street through the nets.

"Have you found her?" Jacob asked, pausing with his spoon halfway to his mouth.

How could she answer that? "I need to speak to you both." She flashed her gaze to Robbie. "Who would like to go first?"

Jacob placed the cheesecake on the sofa arm and stood. "Me. Robbie needs a bit more time."

"I'm afraid that's something we don't have." Helena left the room, opening a door farther down. A bedroom, the one Jacob had been using. The blue bedding was in disarray, one pillow bearing the dent of his head.

She held the door open, and Jacob shuffled past, his eyes red, cheeks blotchy. The civilian in her wanted to hug him, but the copper told her to keep her distance. Andy went in next, and while Jacob plopped onto the bed, she closed the door.

She remained in front of it. Andy stood by the window, glancing out.

"Tell me the order of events this morning from your point of view," Helena said.

Jacob massaged his temples in a circular motion. "I woke up early to knocking. I don't know what time it was, because I don't have a watch, and that copper took my phone. But it was dark, I know that. The knock sounded far away, so I didn't think anything of it and went back to sleep right away. Next thing I know, there's Clive at the door right there, asking me if

193

I've seen Suzie. I haven't seen her since we came here—I left her to it because I was upset and didn't want her worrying about me. What's going on?"

Helena chose to ignore his question. "Is there anything else you can think of that might be relevant?"

He shook his head, twisting his fingers in the hem of his white T-shirt. "No. Like I said, the knocking, but I zonked out again."

"Do you know whether a tartan blanket, a pink bowl, and strawberries has anything to do with Suzie?"

"What the fucking hell are you on about?" He stared at her as though she'd gone mad.

"Okay. We'll leave it there. If you can go and ask Robbie to come in?"

Jacob left the room, and a moment later, Robbie appeared, going to stand by Andy. Was he looking for Suzie outside, hoping she'd walk down the street? God, what an utter shame.

"Robbie, can you tell me a bit about your family's movements last night and this morning, please?"

He didn't turn to face her. "We had a takeaway. Kelvin ordered one in for us. Chinese. Then we bathed the kids, and they went to bed at eight. They were good, which is unusual. I think they're keeping quiet because they know something's going on."

Helena waited while he scrubbed a hand through his hair.

"We watched a bit of telly," he said. "Some documentary, and although I say watched, we didn't really. It was on for background noise. Suzie was upset about Callie and Emma, and she had a good cry. At one point, she mumbled something like, 'He's not going to stop...' I asked her what she meant by that, and she said, 'I just want this to stop.' It wasn't what she'd said at all, but I didn't push her. I thought she might tell me in her own time later down the line."

"Do you have any idea who 'he' is?" Helena asked, excitement building at possibly having a lead.

"No bloody clue, but I got the feeling she knows something. Like, why didn't she tell me about the nail varnish and flowers? Why would she have kept that from me? Wouldn't that be something she would have told me?" He pinched his chin.

Helena couldn't help him there. "What happened then?"

"We went to bed about ten. I stayed awake until I knew Suzie was asleep. I didn't want to drop off and leave her awake in case she needed me to talk to. That was around eleven. My eyes were drooping about twelve, so I went to sleep. We both tossed and turned—her fidgeting woke me up, and I was worried she was going through it a bit, you know, being upset. Last time I checked my watch it was four. I slept again, then Clive came in, asking if we were all right, and I saw Suzie wasn't in bed. Oh Christ…" He hiccoughed a sob.

"Take your time."

He took a deep breath, blowing it out for what seemed ages. "We looked around the flat, but she wasn't there. The kids woke up, what with us making a noise, and Clive told me to wait inside while he went to see Jacob. I was in the kitchen and spotted Clive out in the garden—he must have gone out there through Jacob's—then he went back in. Next thing I know, he's outside in the lobby. I listened at the front door, and he called it in that Suzie was missing and mentioned blood on the path. He wouldn't tell me what it was about. What the hell am I meant to think? My head's a fucking mess."

Helena swallowed. "Are you *sure* no one has a grudge against the sisters?"

"No! I'm at a loss." His bottom lip wobbled, and his red eyes watered.

Poor bastard.

"Does a tartan blanket, a pink bowl, and strawberries mean anything to you or Suzie?"

"Are you having a sodding laugh?" He frowned. "Sorry. God. Listen, I'm really sorry, okay? I'm in bits here."

"Will you sit down, Robbie?" she asked gently, holding out her hand to indicate the bed.

"I can't sit. I need to watch out for Suzie coming back."

"She's not coming back," Helena said.

"What do you mean?" His mouth hung open.

"I'm so very sorry to have to tell you, but we found Suzie's body in the field out the back."

"What?" He blinked, over and over, tears spilling. His face crumpled, cheeks going red, then immediately white, and he staggered to the bed, lowering himself onto the edge. "I don't…I don't understand what you're saying."

Andy glanced at Helena, and it seemed this was getting to him. Too much emotion. Too much to happen to one family.

"She's deceased, Robbie," Helena said. "Again, I'm so sorry."

"Dead? What, did she wander off out there and get cold? That hypothermia thing?"

"I'm afraid not." She bloody hated this part. "She was murdered."

"Eh?" He clutched at his hair, pulling it hard. "Who? Why? I don't…I can't…" Robbie shook his head and shot to his feet. He paced. "I just saw her in the night. It can't be her. Are you sure it's Suzie? Why would she go outside when she knows someone killed her sisters?"

"Yes, we're sure, and I don't know why she'd have gone out there," Helena said. "It's something we'll be looking into. We have so much to piece together. None of this makes sense to us either, so I understand why you're confused." She paused, watching Robbie for signs of an imminent breakdown.

"Shit. The boys…" He rushed out of the room.

Helena and Andy went after him and entered the living room. Robbie leant over the table between his sons, his arms around them, sobbing. The poor kids appeared bewildered, and Helena turned to Jacob.

"What's going on?" he asked.

"It's Suzie," Robbie said.

"Come into the kitchen, Jacob." She berated herself for suggesting that room.

He came in after her and Andy. It was dark, what with the blind and curtain blocking the sun, so she flicked on the light then shut the door.

Round two.

"I'm so sorry, Jacob, but Suzie's body has been found." She clasped her hands in front of her.

"No," he said. "No, that can't be right."

"I'm afraid it is. She was murdered." Pissing hell, would this ever get any easier?

He plopped down onto a chair at the table, shaking his head in disbelief.

"I apologise for asking again, but the blanket..."

"What colour was it?" he asked. Clearly, he was abrupt when upset.

"Red and green."

He closed his eyes. "We had one of those when we used to go on picnics as kids, but I don't see why that's relevant now."

"And the pink bowl and strawberries?" *Come on, Jacob, give me something.*

He nodded and opened his eyes. "Mum had pink Tupperware bowls. The strawberries... We'd gone to the beach. You know that bit down there where it's grass, then it gives way to shingle? There. That's where we were."

"Okay. Did anything significant happen?"

He scrunched his eyebrows. "Yeah. I'd forgotten about it until you just asked, but Suzie went a bit weird."

"What do you mean?"

"She'd gone for a walk to look for some crabs—Dad told her there wouldn't be any, but she had to go and see for herself. The beach bends—you know the part I mean?"

Helena nodded.

"She was gone for a while, but she came running back, frightened-looking, and Dad asked what was wrong, and Suzie burst out crying and said nothing was up. I just thought she was being a bit dramatic, know what I mean? My sisters were prone to theatrics at times. Crying for no reason."

"So she never revealed what had happened?"

"No, but she didn't want to go back there for a picnic again, I know that much."

"Were other people around?"

"There were loads. Plenty of families on the grass bit, plus on the shingle."

"Okay. Thank you. Dave will stay with you for a while, okay? Any questions, ask him. We need to get off now so we can continue the investigation. If you think of anything, tell Dave. He'll get a message to me, okay?"

"Do we still have to stay here?"

"Yes, for the time being. We have no idea what will happen. This person may try again."

"Kill me, you mean."

Helena didn't answer.

He got up and returned to the living room. Helena followed to find Dave. He was on the sofa, one of the lads on his lap. The other sat with Robbie on the chair at the table.

"We're off now," she said and, unable to stand seeing this broken family a minute longer, she left the flat.

Out in the lobby, she leant against the wall next to Clive. Andy did the same beside her, and she stared at the stairs that led to the upper flats. A PC came down, and guilt twitched in Helena's gut at her thought: *Please, don't talk to me. Just give me a second to process this.* However, the officer came up to her.

"Got some news?" she asked, weary.

"No one heard anything," he said. "I'm just going out to help with the other house enquiries."

"Okay, thanks. If you get something, let Clive know, all right?"

He nodded, put gloves on so he didn't touch the door, then disappeared out into the street.

"You told them then?" Clive asked.

"Yes." She didn't have any more words in her.

Gathering her last reserves of energy, she put on fresh booties and gloves, as did Andy, then pointed at Suzie's door. Clive unlocked it. Helena and Andy stepped inside, greeted with the sight of a swarm of SOCOs filling the rooms. She surmised Zach had arrived as well, so she went through the kitchen into the garden. More SOCOs were doing their thing, and she climbed through the now bigger gap in the fence and headed towards the tent that had been erected.

"Something happened to her on that beach," she said to Andy.

"I thought the same. But is it related to this mess?"

"No idea. Maybe we'll never know."

They reached the tent, and Helena pulled the flap aside and entered. Zach was crouching beside Suzie, and he looked up.

"Morning." He smiled, and it was as though they were just work colleagues, nothing more.

Helena was glad. She couldn't be doing with any weirdness when they worked together. "Not a good one."

"No. I may as well get straight to the point. She was stabbed in the lung from the back—the knife punctured through to the front. And also, which is obvious, she had her throat slit. Estimated time of death, which is ballsed up because it's so cold, anywhere from five this morning until eight. I can't get any closer to that at the moment, I'm afraid."

"Where have the bowl and strawberries gone?"

"Tom took them. He sent someone off to deliver them to the lab—better to get them down there as soon as possible."

"Good."

"There's a braided piece of grass here that I found after Tom went back into the garden," Zach said, pointing to it.

Helena frowned. "That's not something you'd normally see. Someone put that there." It was resting beside Suzie, close to her thigh.

"Yep, this person likes leaving gifts."

Helena sighed. "Anything else?"

"Unfortunately, yes." Zach peeled her pyjama top up.

"Oh fuck."

"I know."

Andy coughed, turned away, and heaved.

Suzie no longer had a navel.

CHAPTER TWENTY

The day was so hot, but being on the beach meant it was cooler, so Dad said. Something about the water making the warmth less intense. Suzie didn't know anything about that. She was sweating and needed a drink.

Mum unpacked the picnic bag, spreading the tartan blanket on the grass. Then she pulled out the lemonade and a stack of beakers. Drinks were poured, and Suzie drank hers down in one go. Callie and Emma sat on the blanket and set up Kerplunk. Mum walked off towards the sea while he, that horrible boy who'd come to live with them, stood staring at Suzie as though he hated her.

"I'm going to look for crabs," she said. That was all she could think of. She'd get away from him then, even if it was just for a little while.

"There won't be any," Dad said. "There never is this time of year. The rock pools dry up in this sun."

"I'm going to see anyway," Suzie said and, after another glare from the boy, she legged it across the grass and around the corner, weaving through other mums and dads, lots of children, and a few grannies.

She headed for where the rock pools usually were and, sure enough, they were dried out. The crabs must have scuttled across the beach and back into the sea. Not wanting to go back yet, she wandered along until the grass led to a stand of tall reeds, higher than her, each reed more than an inch thick with dried-out edges. She went behind it and sat, alone at last, but the shrieks and laughter from those on the shingle let her know people weren't too far away.

She was safe here.

She ripped a piece of reed at the base and peeled it into three strips, then tied a knot in the ends and plaited them. Every so often, she gazed up at the cliff. Finished with her plait, she made it into a necklace and put it on.

A shadow fell over the grass, person-shaped, legs apart, arms akimbo. She knew that shape, the broadness, the absolute size of him. Suzie kept her head down.

"A circle signifies never-ending love, so I was told," he said. "Well, a wedding ring does anyway. Wasn't much cop for my mum and dad, was it."

She didn't need him telling her useless things. He was always showing off at the dinner table, going on about stuff no one cared about except for Mum and

Dad. They seemed to like it and encouraged him. Why he couldn't go and live with someone else, she didn't know. She hated him.

His arm came into her line of vision, and he snatched the grass necklace off her. It hurt a bit from the pressure before it snapped. He crouched and tickled her face with the end, then moved it lower.

"At one of the foster places I lived in," he said, swirling the plait over her skin, "the mum had a thing about flowers. She had red rose bushes, pink tulips, and loads of these little lilac ones called forget-me-nots – that's your flower, that one. She used to go and make me pick them for her when she wanted some in the house. Every time I did it, she hit me for picking her flowers."

Suzie didn't care. He'd probably picked them without being asked and was making it look like the mum was mean.

"Then her husband used to come into my room that night and paint my nails."

Suzie glanced up at him then, because she'd swear it sounded as though he was crying. His face was as obscure as his shadow, though, what with the sun beaming from behind him and directly in her eyes.

"Go away," she said, the memory of him coming into the cupboard under the stairs flashing through her mind.

"Don't tell me what to do," he said. "You know what will happen if you don't do as you're told."

"You didn't tell me I had to be nice to you."

"Well, now you do. New rule."

She got up and pushed past him, running back towards her family, crying until she thought her heart would break. She slowed, swiping at her eyes, and watched her sisters giggling, Jacob and Dad playing cards, and Mum doling out the pink bowls ready to fill them with strawberries from their fruit patch back home.

"What's up, love?" Dad asked, frowning.

She couldn't tell him, otherwise he'd be dead.

"Nothing," she said, then burst into tears again.

"No crabs?" he asked.

"No."

She plonked down on the blanket beside Jacob, grabbing his arm and hugging it, his skin hot on her wet cheek. The horrible boy came back and sat opposite her. While they all ate their strawberries, he stared at her, and she thought that stare might just break her in two it was that hard.

CHAPTER TWENTY-ONE

Helena sat on the edge of Andy's desk to address her team. "Got anything for me?"

Olivia held up her pen. "The kids went to Smaltern Primary then Secondary. I've looked into their classmates—not quite done with that—and a few of them are on each of their social media friends lists. Some of the women are married, so that's why I haven't finished. I'm in the middle of matching maiden names to married."

"Okay, the next step will be to contact them and ask a few questions. I'll leave that to you," Helena said. "Phil?"

"The camera outside the flats doesn't show anyone hanging around during the night, so we'd have to assume they came from the back."

Helena nodded. "Easily done." She explained the layout of the fields, copse, and the broken fence.

"The camera in the lobby outside the safe flats, though…" Phil winced.

"Don't tell me it was a fucking resident," Helena said.

"No. Have a look at this."

Phil turned his monitor so they could all see it. Helena walked closer. He brought up a window, and a clear image of Kelvin sitting outside the flat doors in the lobby, illuminated from the overhead strip light, filled the screen.

"He's asleep!" Helena all but shouted. "Bloody wonderful! He's there to keep them safe, and he's having a sodding kip!" She stared at the ceiling. "He's so in the shit for this. Yarworth will have his bollocks on a plate."

Andy grunted. "Yeah, the chief only comes out of the woodwork to dish out grief." He glanced over his shoulder as though expecting Yarworth to appear and give him a rollocking.

Helena was steaming angry. "Someone got killed because of Kelvin. If he'd been awake, he might have heard Suzie go outside and checked what was going on."

"I wouldn't want to be him when he finds out he's been caught sleeping on the job," Phil said.

"And the little shit said to Clive nothing was amiss." Helena thumped her thigh. "*God.* He'd better not come anywhere near me. I'm likely to punch the twat. Give me two minutes." She stormed to her office and flopped into her chair, more incensed than she'd ever been, even more than when Uthway and his buddy had treated her the way they had.

Suzie was dead because of incompetence. Kelvin had blood on his hands, and all because he hadn't been able to stay awake. She understood the monotony of lonely night shifts, but with this case being *so* important, he should have got up and paced or something. Jesus!

Blowing out a shivering breath, she closed her eyes and forced herself to calm down. They had so much to do and nothing to go on. How did you find a killer who was so clever?

She stalked back to the incident room. "Right. Anything else that might get my back up today?"

Olivia bit her lip. "The Walkers were foster parents."

"Oh, for fu—" Helena thought about the streams of children who would have been through their household over the years. Could it be one of them? "Okay. And?"

"They only fostered one kid, a lad called Franklin Marston."

Why does that name ring a bell? "Right…"

"He stayed with them for almost ten years. He moved in when he was thirteen in ninety-six."

"What's that make him now?" Helena couldn't get her brain to work.

"Thirty-six."

"And where is he these days?"

"That's just it," Olivia said. "He went off the radar about ten years ago. He's got a few priors, nothing too bad. Stealing and the like."

"Deed Poll?"

"That's next on my list."

"Okay, get on that—forget the classmates for now. Andy, you and me need to go back and talk to Jacob. Why the hell didn't he mention this Franklin? Ten years he was there. It's not something you're likely to bloody forget is it?"

She left the room and headed to the car park, rage building again. What was the problem with this family? Emma hadn't wanted to talk about whatever was bothering her, Suzie had lied, and the pair of them and Jacob had left a massive chunk of their childhood out by not saying about Franklin Marston. Robbie hadn't said a word either.

In the car, she gripped the steering wheel and rested her forehead on her knuckles. If she didn't get a handle on herself, she was likely to say something she'd regret once they arrived at the flats.

Andy got in and squeezed her shoulder. "We'll just sit for a minute or two, if you like."

She sat back. "What's the matter with these people?"

"I'm as stumped as you. Maybe Jacob didn't think this Franklin was important."

"What? He shared a decade of his life with him. Do they still see him? Is he in the nick? Is he dead? Is it him doing this?" Her stomach growled, fuck it. "And we haven't eaten since we were at the gym."

"Sandwich on the go?"

She nodded and started the engine, driving to the local garage. Andy took her proffered twenty.

"Get something for Clive as well, will you?"

Andy disappeared inside the garage, coming back with manky-looking cheese sandwiches and cans of Coke.

She stared at the Coke. "Really?"

"What?"

"You could at least have got diet."

"Be quiet. You're turning into me, always moaning."

She smiled and opened her sandwich carton, then drove away, eating as she went. She'd finished by the time they reached the flats. In the lobby, she handed Clive his lunch. "Kelvin fell asleep." Might as well be blunt about it.

Clive reared his head back, eyebrows climbing upwards. "Oh."

"Can you let us in, please." She was impatient to get this oversight cleared up, although 'oversight' was a bloody stretch.

She walked into the flat, and once again, Dave poked his head out of the living room doorway. She entered when he stepped back to let her in.

"Jacob, we need to talk to you again." She'd sounded abrupt, but it was too late to change it now.

He shuffled behind her into the kitchen, and Andy closed the door. He leant against it, probably to give his poor gym legs a rest.

Jacob sat at the table, resting his elbows on top. He wheezed a bit, and Helena wondered if he had asthma like Suzie.

"Are you all right?" she asked.

"As well as I can be in this sort of situation." He tsked.

She realised her mistake. "No, I meant the wheezing."

"Oh. Yeah. It's fine. Have you found something?"

Helena folded her hands over her stomach. "Two words: Franklin Marston."

Jacob scowled, and he shifted from side to side, probably uncomfortable beneath her stare. He wiped his mouth with the back of his hand. Or was that his sweating top lip? "What about him?" The words came out gruff, as though he was annoyed at being caught withholding information.

"Why didn't you, Suzie, or Emma tell me about him? He was part of your family."

"He's a nasty piece of shit, that's what he is." He huffed, lips wobbling with the exhalation.

"Do you still see him?" she asked.

"From time to time. He shows up, I tell him to sling his hook."

"Why?"

"Can't stand him."

"What did your sisters think of him?"

"They tolerated him. He visited them more than me." His face told a story—that he didn't like Franklin seeing his sisters.

"Where does he live?"

"I don't know."

"Pardon?" Surely he had to be kidding here.

"I don't *know*!" He tunnelled his fingers through his hair.

"Does he work?"

"I don't talk to him about anything like that. I try not to talk about him at all. When he moved in, things changed. I had to share a room with him, and he was…weird. Scary. So much bigger than us. Like a man. I was younger than him, and he was this thirteen-year-old beefcake who had a massive chip on his shoulder. He used to tell me at night, when we were in bed, that I had everything he wished he had, and if I didn't do what he wanted, he'd take my family away from me."

Helena fought the urge to scream. "So when I asked you if anyone had a grudge, and you said no, you didn't think that snippet of information was important? That someone basically threatening to take your family away wasn't linked to your family *actually being taken away*?"

"I didn't think of it like that."

He hasn't thought much at all!

"You have no one left apart from Robbie and the boys, Jacob," she said. "It seems this Franklin has done exactly what he said he'd do. What if he extends that threat to those little lads? What then?"

"I didn't—"

"No, you didn't think. We've established that bit. What did he want you to do?"

"Pinch money off our dad." Jacob flushed. "I'm not proud of that, but he forced me to do it. I believed him when he said he'd kill everyone. I took money out of Dad's wallet, and Franklin bought booze and fags. He looked old enough, so it didn't surprise me the first time he came back with a stash."

"So when your dad died…?"

"That was my fault. I said I wouldn't steal anymore, then Dad had the car accident. The brakes were faulty."

Helena's inner alarm went off. "Why wasn't that investigated more thoroughly by the police?"

"It was, but they didn't do anything. It was borderline. Like, they couldn't prove they'd been actually messed with, but I know they were. It was *him*. He fucking *said* so, the bastard. 'See what I did, twat?' That's what he said."

This bloke here had been comfort eating for years, blaming himself for his father's death, when some cretin teenager had possibly done it.

"Okay, I'm going to get someone to check the details on that. If you think Franklin had something to do with the brakes…"

Jacob shrugged.

Helena sighed. "So, I'm going to ask you again, and please, *please* don't keep anything back from me now. Do you know where Franklin lives?"

"No!" He paused, then, "He used to sneak out of our room at night and go into the girls'. He'd be in there for a bit, then I'd hear him opening the back door. I looked out the window. He always stood drinking a beer, a fag in the other hand. He did it every time he'd been in there."

"Did your sisters say why he'd gone in their room?"

"They said he didn't, but I know he did. His voice came through the wall."

Helena's stomach hurt from tensing her muscles. What did Franklin need to go into the girls' room for? Her mind went to a dark place, and she shoved the thoughts away. They came back, though, with something she needed to find out. "Did the flowers appear outside their bedrooms before or after Franklin moved in?"

Jacob frowned, clearly searching his memory bank. "I was eight when I got the red toy car, and Franklin was there then, because he was a wanker at my birthday party. He broke one of my presents—a Power Ranger figure. He snapped the arms and legs off. Said that'd be me if I opened my mouth about him telling me to nick the money."

Christ. It was looking likely this foster kid was a nasty little shit who'd sadly gone down the wrong path because of his upbringing.

"Anything else you can think of that might help us?" she asked.

"The hamster was strangled, so the vet said."

Oh. Now this was getting text book. And disturbing. "After Franklin's arrival?"

"Yeah. He must have done it in the night, although I didn't hear him opening the cage. If you let me go home, he might turn up at mine, then I can let you know he's there, and you can come and ask him some questions."

She wanted to do more than that, like kick his head in, but funny enough, Yarworth would frown on that. "No. You have to stay here. There is no way we can allow you to leave yet. Don't worry, your boss has been informed of your sisters' passing. Just hang tight, and we'll do our best."

"Be careful. He's a nasty piece of work."

"What does he look like?" She glanced at Andy: *write this down.*

"About six-two, built like a brick shithouse. Dark hair, although he dyes it. Got to, because he was blond as a kid and until about ten years ago. He must do his eyebrows and all."

"Thanks. We'll be in touch. Take care of yourself, okay?"

He nodded.

Helena walked out of the flat. She got the latest from Clive, which was nothing more than what they already knew, then she and Andy went back to the station. There was a lot of sifting through data to do, and she intended to help out. If all four of them were searching, they'd find the information quicker.

Andy went to his desk, and Helena made everyone a coffee. After an update from Olivia and Phil, she settled at a spare desk, booted up the computer, and got to work. With a phone number found for the local social services, she lifted the phone to give a Mrs Featherstone a ring.

"Hi, I'm Detective Inspector Stratton, and I'm calling regarding a child who was in the system. I realise you might not be able to give me details, but I'm going to ask anyway."

"It depends what you want to know," Mrs Featherstone said.

"I'm working on a triple murder enquiry, and we need to speak to a man urgently. His name is Franklin Marston, and he went to live with the Walker family in ninety-six when he was thirteen. Smaltern. My colleague has tracked his National Insurance number, but it stopped appearing in the records a decade ago. She's been trying to find out whether he changed his name, but if he did, he didn't apply for an Enrolled Deed Poll from the Ministry of Justice, so it isn't on public record. Sadly, the lady at the office wouldn't hand out any information without a warrant. We're waiting for one now. However, I'm chancing my arm here to see if you can possibly email me an image of Franklin Marston, just so I know who I'm looking for."

"*Triple* murder?"

"Unfortunately, yes. The three daughters in the Walker family. We have the fourth sibling, a son, in a safe house at the minute. Some information has come to light that means I really do need to speak with Franklin as soon as possible."

"Is he a suspect?"

Forgive me for lying... "Not at present, no. I need information about the time he was living with the family. He may remember something that might help us with the investigation."

"I shouldn't really, not without a —"

"Warrant, I know."

"But..." Mrs Featherstone sighed. "A picture won't hurt, will it?"

"No, that's all I need. Thank you so much." Helena rattled off her email address then ended the call. She logged in to her account, butterflies wreaking havoc inside her at the thought of seeing the possible killer. They were getting somewhere, at last.

Her email pinged, and she clicked on the one from Mrs Featherstone. She hovered the cursor over the image attachment icon and pressed down on the mouse. A photo loaded. A blond kid who looked about eighteen, although she thought about what Jacob had said and realised this picture had probably been taken around the time he'd gone to live with the Walkers. She imagined him with dark hair and eyebrows.

Her stomach plummeted, and her mouth went dry. It couldn't be *him*, could it? He certainly looked similar, but lots of people did, didn't they? She rummaged in her mind, sorting through their conversations for any little sign he'd let something slip.

Nothing.

She rang Clive. "Can you put Jacob on, please." She had a question that would clear this up once and for all. If Jacob answered a certain way, she'd know for sure.

A few seconds passed, then, "Hello?"

"Jacob, it's Helena. Does Franklin ever wear anything that would make him stand out?"

"What, like a fucking mac and a fedora? Yeah."

Helena's blood ran cold. She ended the call, hand shaking as she placed the phone down. Her head flooded with images of him and how easily she could have been Suzie, Emma, and Callie. She breathed deep and closed her eyes until her heartrate slowed.

Then it was time to find Marshall.

CHAPTER TWENTY-TWO

*H*e'd found her. The hated foster mother with the garden full of flowers. He'd left the Walker home now, living by himself in a rented two-up, two-down. An adult. No longer under the regimes of those so-called carers of his youth. Although the Walker parents had been good to him, he'd never fitted in. Always the outsider, despite the mum and dad trying to include him in everything, he'd wandered through those years under their care with hate twisting his heart and a demon eating his soul bit by bit.

He'd learnt a trade, though, tiling, so their encouragement had helped with something. Shame it hadn't healed him. Fixed him.

He stood in her front garden, and the mad urge to rip up all her fucking flowers stroked him, an unseen hand that pushed him on the back towards the roses, the tulips, and the forget-me-nots. He picked one of each and held them behind his back while he rang the bell.

She answered, an old lady now, hair white and wispy, skin weathered with spite, all the times she'd scowled or frowned mapped out on her skin, lines of her abuse telling the tale of a life lived mired in hatred.

He'd lived the same life. What you reaped, you sowed, and on it went down the generations if your tendencies weren't caught soon enough.

"What do you want?" she asked, peering at him through thick-lens glasses, her once bright-blue eyes that had rivalled a summer sky dulled to thunder grey. She still had that dreadful eyeshadow on. Shiny blue. "I don't buy nothing on the doorstep."

"I'm not selling," he said. "I'm here to check your pipes under the kitchen sink. Council reported a leak." He lifted his royal-blue holdall, the business end of a hammer poking out through the not-quite-closed zip.

Her lips flapped, words failing her, and she glanced to the side and up, thinking, clearly struggling to recall whether she had a leak or not. He dropped his bag and produced a card from his pocket using his free hand. He flashed a mocked-up identity badge, laminated to appear real.

"Tsk, fucking come in then," she said. "Pain up the bloody arse, this is."

She stepped back into the hallway, and he grabbed his bag, entering the house he'd been beaten in as a *kid. It still resembled the interior of the past, although thirty years ago it had been new wallpaper and paint. Now it peeled and flaked, some hanging down at the top corner by the banister rail. Her nail-painting freak of a husband obviously wasn't here anymore to do the handiwork. Or if he was, he was too old.*

He closed the door while she shuffled off down the hall. Then he peered into the living room – no one there.

Good.

In the kitchen, she stood by the sink, pulling one of the cabinet doors open. "There you go."

He smiled at her. "Where's George?"

She blinked. "What's it got to do with you, nosy beak?" Her face scrunched up. "'Ere, how did you know my old man's name?"

"Live on your own now, do you?" he asked, anger uncoiling inside him; she still spoke the same way. Rude. Abrupt. No respect. No manners.

"You need to mind your own fucking business and get on with fixing that ruddy pipe," she said, pointing at it with a gnarled finger, the knuckles bulbous.

He brought the flowers out from behind his back. She stared at them for a moment, eyes glassy, as though she peeked back in time at what the flowers represented.

"Did you beat all the kids who picked these for you, or just me?" He tilted his head and forced her to make eye contact.

"Which one of them little bastards are you?" She sucked in her bottom lip.

"Franklin Marston."

"Ah, him. Worst of the lot, you were. Always picking my flowers." She flicked her gaze to the ones he held out. "Some things never change."

"You asked me to pick them, then you beat me."

"So what if I did?" She thumped her fists onto her hips.

He placed the bag on the worktop and drew out the hammer, putting the flowers on the draining board.

Then he staved her head in.

Afterwards, he stared at her crumpled body on the lino, then let his gaze drift over the room. The little dining table had material on it, a rich velvet, burgundy. Beside it sat a sewing kit, the case open like a book, needles in one side, tiny spools of thread in the other.

He sewed up her mouth with black cotton so she couldn't say hateful things ever again. Black for her ebony heart. Rested the flowers on her chest. And painted her nails with different colours.

Red. Pink. Purple.

He took the sewing kit with him, a sense of peace flowing through his soul for the first time since he could remember.

In his new car outside the back of the police station, parked in a long line of vehicles, he reflected on earlier this morning. He stroked his sewing kit while holding it against his chest. It gave him so much comfort. It had been there from his first time, and while he held it, he experienced the same peace.

Seeing Helena at the leisure centre with that Andy bloke had brought on anger so fierce he hadn't been able to think straight. He shouldn't have done that neck-slicing gesture, though. She was a strong woman and wouldn't take it lightly. He'd thought she was The One, the person to help him raise a family, to mend everything that was broken inside him. To be the kind of father to their children he'd never had.

Once she'd gone inside, he'd driven to the flats—him tailing the car that had taken Suzie and Jacob there had been worth it. Following Helena also had its advantages. He'd known, when he'd approached her in The Blue Pigeon that first night, who she was and that she would deal with any murder investigations. She hadn't remembered, but she'd nicked him in her rookie days. When he'd been blond. When he'd been Franklin Marston. When she'd had long hair instead of the short cut she had now. He'd banked on her forgetting the arrest, and she had. He hadn't banked on her finishing with him, though. He'd planned to pick her brains every time he killed one of the Walkers, encouraging her to spill information he might need to know in order to remain off the radar.

Still, he'd managed it so far without her, so that was a bonus.

The picnic blanket, bowl, strawberries, and plaited reed had been a nice touch. While they'd eaten on the beach all those years ago, he'd enjoyed staring at Suzie. Frightening her. Silently bending her to his will. Once he'd killed her, he'd placed the things inside her then sewed her up, using the purple thread that was so Suzie. He'd done it by the light of the torch app on one of his phones after he'd laid her out on the grass under the silent, reproachful gaze of the trees standing sentinel beside them.

His run along the path had led him to an alley, and he'd dipped into it, slowing to a walk on the housing estate. Gulls had squawked in the distance, and a meek sun had risen, turning the black sky to a browny-grey. Someone had come out of a house and got into their car, on the way to work, he'd reckoned. He'd clamped his arms over the bloodstain on his mac, thankful it was still murky enough for the wet patch not to show.

Home again, he'd shoved the mac in the wash then showered, off out once more to tail Helena.

Ah, there she was. She shot up the road, and he followed at a steady pace, allowing another car to come between them at one point. On she went, through the town centre, then turning right onto an industrial estate. Down a winding road, she indicated right and stopped outside Tim's Tiles.

His workplace. Why had he told her he worked there?

He carried on, going to the end and parking, engine idling, facing the way he'd come so he could watch what happened next. She was probably there to serve him with that fucking restraining order, or did they come in the post? Fingers of anger clutched at his belly, and his cheeks grew hot, itchy. It shouldn't have come to this. They should still be together, her letting him move in; they could have been a family then.

Why had he got nasty with her over his mac and hat that time when she'd laughed? Why hadn't he just brushed off what she'd said? She'd known, then, he wasn't who he'd made himself out to be. She'd glimpsed the demon inside.

Suzie's belly button lay heavy in his stomach. The navel, a symbol of having been born and of giving life. The special link between a mother and child. He'd cut it out from jealousy. Her bratty sons didn't deserve a woman like her. She'd let herself go to pot since she'd had them, her lovely figure becoming disguised, heavier.

Or had she let the weight pile on so he wouldn't want to go near her again?

Why would he once she'd been with Robbie?

Same with the other two. They were all soiled.

Helena's car nudged over the intersection line, and she drove back down the winding road. He gave chase, and they ended up in his street. He'd called in sick since he'd killed Callie, so his boss had probably told her that. Wow, she really did want to hand him that order personally.

Bitch.

While she parked on his drive, he slid his car between a silver Ford and a bubblegum-blue Fiat. Helena and Andy got out and walked up his path. She knocked on the door with the side of her fist, and Andy peered through the living room window. Helena bent down and pushed the letterbox in.

He opened the car window.

"Marshall?" she called. "Franklin Marston, open this door!"

His skin rippled with goosebumps, and his heart thumped wildly. He hadn't heard or used that name in years, but somehow, she'd found out who he was. Had she done so because of the restraining order? Deed Poll weren't supposed to share your old name. What the fuck was going on?

She knocked on the door again, and Andy went down the alley at the side of the house, while Helena stepped back and stared up at the bedroom window. He'd fucked her in there, so she knew the layout. She was checking whether he was upstairs in his room, peering down at her.

Crafty cow.

Andy returned, shaking his head, and they chatted quietly, heads together. Helena nodded, then they left his place and walked to the next-door neighbour's. He stared in fury, riled up beyond measure—they were messing with his life, and there was nothing he could do about it.

Or was there?

Helena pressed the bell and waited. The door swung open. A woman of about thirty stood there, a boy standing beside her, clamped to her leg. He was two, give or take a few months. His fingers, covered in flour, left white marks on her black jeans.

"Yes?" she asked.

Helena showed her ID. "Sorry to bother you, but do you know your neighbour?" She pointed to Marshall's house.

"Oh, I remember you," she said. "You used to go there sometimes at night."

Helena hoped she didn't blush. To be reminded that she'd had a relationship with a man who might have killed set her teeth on edge. "Do you know him well?"

"No. He doesn't speak. I tried waving once, but he didn't return it."

"Have you seen anything suspicious around here regarding him? I'm sorry, what's your name?"

"Laura Brown. And if you mean him coming in and out at all hours lately, then yes."

"What sorts of times?"

"Let me see. The other night it was late, after twelve. The night after was long past two. This morning, he went out early and came back around two hours later. He wears this weird mac and hat. Really creepy."

Helena had found it funny when she'd seen it the first time, but it wasn't amusing now. "Okay. How did you know he'd come back so late?"

Laura pointed at her child's head. "He's a light sleeper. I'd go round to next door and ask him to be quiet but I find him a bit weird. Don't want to risk him shouting at me or whatever." She pressed a finger to her chin. "He either talks to himself or shouts at someone on the phone. I'm leaning more towards the first one."

"What do you mean?"

"Well, if he hasn't got anyone in his house — that I know of anyway — why would I hear a two-sided convo?"

Marshall hadn't struck Helena as the type to do something like that, but if she were honest, she didn't know him, not really. "What sort of thing does he say?"

"Well, if it's him doing both people's voices, he talks really deep and calls himself Mr Jeffs, saying stuff like, 'You'll never be the man in the house, you horrible little scrote!' Then as himself, he says stuff I'd rather not repeat." She pointed to her son again.

Andy held out his notebook and pen. "Write it down for us."

Laura did, her boy toddling off farther inside the house, clearly bored. She handed the book to Helena.

You need to watch your fucking mouth, or I'll have you.

Helena glanced at Andy, then back at Laura. "Okay, thanks for that. Anything else you can help us with?"

"Can I ask why you want to know?" Laura rubbed the flour off her jeans. "Do I need to be worried?"

"Let's just say don't speak to him, and if he comes here, don't open the door. Here's my card," Helena said. "If you get any bother or see him come home, ring me immediately."

"Okay…"

"Thanks for your time. You've been very helpful."

Laura smiled and closed the door, and Helena led the way to the car.

"Mr Jeffs," she said once they were inside and buckling up. She handed him back his notebook. "A split personality or a real person?" She rang Olivia. "Can you look up all men called Jeffs, please, connected to Franklin. We're heading back now, so I'll pick the info up when we're at the station."

Pissed off at being unable to get into Marshall's house without a warrant, she backed out of his drive and sped off. "What on earth is going on here?"

"Beats me," Andy said. "Are you okay?"

"Why wouldn't I be?" She knew why he was asking but was desperate to make out she was fine.

"Well, with Franklin being Marshall."

"I'll have to be," she said. "As you know, I've been through much worse. Maybe I'm lucky to be alive. If it's him doing this, he could very well want to kill me."

CHAPTER TWENTY-THREE

As soon as they drove off, he knocked on his neighbour's door. She opened it right away, as though she thought Helena and Andy had come back. Her face showed her shock with its open mouth and eyebrows shooting up.

"Oh, it's you," she said.

"Can I come in for a minute?" He lifted the knife that had been down by his side and held it in front of him, the end pointing at her. It still had Suzie's blood on it.

"Oh God…" She moved to slam the door, his boot in the way preventing her from managing it.

"Not a good idea. I just want to talk, all right?" He tilted his head and smiled.

She nodded, stepping back, and ran down the hallway into her kitchen. He stepped inside and closed the door, following her. She was by the washing machine, picking her son up, then rushed to the back door and flung it open. She dashed outside and screamed.

He stood at the back door, frowning. "Really no need for that," he called over the racket she was making. He shook his head. "Come back in. I just want to know what they wanted."

She shut up and backed to the fence at the bottom. It reminded him of dragging Suzie through the one at the flats.

"I have a child. Please don't hurt us." Her eyes were massive through fear.

"What did they want? Answer, and I'll leave."

She opened the back gate and reversed through.

Fuck.

He chased her down the alley at the back of the houses, speeding up when it was obvious she'd come out at the end of the street onto a busy thoroughfare where people might see them. But she was whippet-fast and made it there before him. She darted forward, into the road. She was there, in the middle, staring to her left, then she was gone, ploughed down by a black SUV.

And he hadn't even needed to get his hands dirty.

He walked back up the alley and into his own back garden, through the house, and out to his car. He had someone he needed to see. Stopping in town to buy a bunch of red roses, he drove to Smaltern Secondary and parked where he usually did whenever he collected Elsa, his latest girl. She reminded him of Callie when she'd been the same age. Although school wasn't even close to finishing, he hoped she'd see him out there through a window.

Five minutes passed.

Out she came and got in, hiding in the back as usual. He drove to their favourite place, the cliff top, and they sat together while he did the things he did to these sorts of girls, then pushed her off the ledge. He couldn't have her blabbing. Others had been dealt with in different ways, but all of them were gone now. He tossed the roses over, the wind crackling the cellophane for a moment before the bunch vanished.

He made his way to Helena's so she'd have a nice surprise when she got home from work. Her back door had always had a dodgy handle, wobbly, and it didn't take him long to break in. He had a relaxing bath using her Avon bubbles, then dried himself with her soft towels. Naked, he rubbed himself all over her furniture, marking it, making sure he was the man in the house.

Then he sat on the sofa and waited.

With the news that Mr Jeffs was deceased — suicide by jumping off a cliff — Helena saw no point in them carrying on with overtime. Two PCs out of uniform had been sent to sit outside Marshall's until he turned up, and with beat officers aware of who they needed to be looking for — Helena had provided them with a picture she'd taken of him while they'd been together — there wasn't much else they could do.

She dropped Andy home and told him to forget the gym in the mornings for now. They were both knackered, so it was best they resumed when this case was over. Hopefully it'd be soon. She stopped off to get herself a cheeky Burger King — bad for her, but shit, she was too tired to care. A bottle of white wine waited in her fridge, so she'd pop that cork after a bath and try to relax.

That might prove difficult. Her mind spun in all directions. She should have told Chief Yarworth that she couldn't continue now she'd discovered Marshall was involved in the case, but she'd never been one to follow the rules that closely and was fucked if she'd let someone else take all the glory for nicking Marshall. And no, she wouldn't even let it be Andy. This was her collar, and she intended to see it through until the end.

Home, she parked up and collected her dinner off the passenger seat, then gratefully went inside, slipping her shoes off beside the door. Her feet and legs ached — probably not as much as Andy's, though. She shut the door then walked into the kitchen, placing her Burger King bag and mobile on the worktop. Wine uncorked, she poured half a glass, knocking it back. It burned on the way down, warming her inside, and that reminded her of the nip in the air. She moved into the hallway to turn the thermostat dial, then opened the living room door, intending to switch on the electric fire to heat the house quicker while she was in the bath.

A naked Marshall sat on her sofa directly opposite the door.

What the fuck?

Stomach flipping, she backed into the hallway, sliding her hand into her pocket for her phone. Shit, it was in the kitchen. Darting in there, she grabbed it and cursed having a bloody PIN to unlock the screen. Marshall came in, thudding towards her, and she reversed to the back door. Yanking the handle, she expected the door to be locked, but it opened. She shot outside and legged it down the garden, but he was there, right behind her, gripping her hair and dragging her backwards.

"Help!" she screamed over and over, her training kicking in. Make noise—lots of it. "Fifteen Vickers Terrace. Call the police!"

He hefted her over the doorstep, and her heels caught on it. She grimaced in pain and gave one last scream, long and loud. Punching at him behind her with her free hand, she glanced down while he hauled her into the living room. She pressed her phone icon for contacts, hit Andy's, and the faint ring meshed with her heavy breathing.

Marshall shoved her onto the sofa, and she dropped her phone between her outer thigh and a scatter cushion. Andy, his voice tinny and far away, asked if she was all right. If she didn't answer, it would be enough to have him come running.

"What are you doing in my house, Marshall?" she said loudly.

"What were you doing at mine?" he said. "At my neighbour's?"

He should have looked ridiculous standing there with no clothes on, but he didn't. It was creepy. She suppressed a shudder.

"I had to deliver a restraining order," she said.

"So why did you call me Franklin Marston? Who is he, I wonder?"

"You tell me." She should have said that nicely, not in such an acerbic way, but it was out there now, floating between them.

"I don't know him anymore," he said.

"Who is Mr Jeffs?" That had come out better. Calm. Non-abrasive. Like they were just having an ordinary natter. She had to switch from her manic behaviour in the garden to a calmer state. Let him think she wasn't mad at him now. That she'd had a sudden change of heart.

He stared at her, eyes widening then narrowing in an instant. She'd let him know she knew more than he thought. Had it been a mistake?

"How do you know about him?" he ground out.

"He came up in a line of enquiry. I have a serial killer on my hands. Look, sit down, will you? And if you can't do that, go and get the wine. I need a drink."

"Don't move," he said and left the room.

I can't believe he fell for it. She picked her phone up. "Andy?" she whispered.

"Backup on the way," he said. "As am I."

"Okay. Back door is open. Got to go."

She put the phone beside her, making sure the lit screen faced the seat cushion. She could have got up, dashed out of the front door, but she wasn't letting this man go. Some would say putting herself in danger was foolhardy, and she'd agree with that, but if it meant getting him arrested, she'd do whatever it took.

Marshall came back in and set the wine bottle and glasses on the coffee table, pouring a measure in each. He took his and sat in one of the armchairs beside the door, probably so he could get up quick if she made a run for it. She reached for her drink and sipped.

"What happened to you?" she asked.

"Long story." He gulped some wine.

"I have time."

"What, are you going to do your police thing on me, is that it? You're going to try to unbreak my mind by a bit of a chat? Doesn't work like that." Sweat broke out on his face, and he tapped his foot, knee bouncing. "Shit, I need my kit."

Kit?

"Go and get it then, if it's here, that is." She crossed her legs. "I'm not going anywhere. I've had a tough day and need a breather after you shitting the life out of me by being here, so you jog on and do what you need to do. Putting on some clothes might be a good idea and all." She flopped her head back and closed her eyes for effect.

A scrape—where he'd put his glass on the table? She sensed him leave, the sound of his footsteps on the stairs confirming it. Opening her eyes, she strained to catch the rumble of cars

242

out the front. All was quiet. A creak came from above—him in her bedroom. She dreaded to think what he'd been doing up there before she'd arrived.

She picked up her phone and whispered, "How long?"

"Five minutes," Andy said.

She placed her mobile beside her just as Marshall came down the stairs. He entered the room in a pair of jeans, swiped up his drink, and sat again. She stared at him pressing a slim, plastic box to his chest. His kit? It wasn't big enough to hold anything much, about the length of his hand.

"All right now?" she asked.

"Bit better."

"Do you want to talk?"

"Not about me. I have a few questions. Why did you end it?"

"We weren't really going anywhere, were we. You'd started to get pissy, if you remember, and I can't be doing with aggro. Your temper gets the better of you—you've got to admit that."

A scowl rippled his forehead, and his face reddened. Was he about to go off on one? She tensed, ready to spring into action, but he relaxed, and his features smoothed out.

"I thought you were it," he said. "You know, the one to fix me."

Bloody hell. He'd thought more about their relationship than she had. To her, they'd just been seeing each other. Fuck-buddies, really, nothing more. Once he'd shown her his darker side, that had been it. Too much hassle. She had enough of her own baggage. Helping him to carry his wasn't something she could manage.

"Sorry I'm not 'it', but we'd never work." She drank some more wine. It helped calm her nerves, which had decided to pipe up about being jangled. "You need a more understanding woman."

"Maybe." He'd said it grudgingly, like he didn't want to admit she was right.

"Why did you pop round anyway?" she asked, as if he hadn't been in her house naked and dragged her by her hair. Best to keep it casual, forgetting, for now, it had even happened. Riling him wouldn't help.

"I needed to see you." He stroked his 'kit'.

"What for?" She held her breath—a car was in the street.

"To kill you."

"Oh." Her legs numbed, and a buzzing set up home in her ears. "That's a shame. Why would you want to do that?"

"I need to be the man in the house, and you wouldn't let me. Said I couldn't move in. I'd planned it, wanted it, but you fucked it all up. You made me do what I've done."

She wasn't falling for that old chestnut, taking the blame for his thoughts and actions. Whatever he'd done was on him, not her. He could fuck right off on that one.

"What do you mean, 'the man in the house'?" she asked, hoping her voice didn't sound as croaky to him as it did to her.

"You wouldn't understand." He continued stroking his kit.

"Try me."

A slight noise of movement caught her attention — out the back, possibly someone walking over the grass.

"No. You need to just shut the hell up." He sprang out of his chair and lunged towards her.

Helena jumped up and moved to the side, and he went headfirst into the sofa. She straddled him from behind, down on her knees, and gripped his wrists, drawing his arms behind his back. With nothing to secure him with, she was stuck there, hoping the noise she'd just heard was help coming. She wouldn't have the strength to keep him in place indefinitely. He bucked, trying to throw her off, and she clung on, clamping her inner thighs against his legs.

"You fucking whore," he said, the words muffled by the seat cushion.

She squeezed his wrists, and his little box fell to the carpet, popping open and displaying the contents. A sewing kit. Her stomach revolted at the sight of the thick needles and threads, cotton so chunky it was the same sort used on the Walker sisters. He lifted his torso, and she reared with him, then he concentrated all his weight on her. Her muscles protested, and she hit the floor, his heaviness on top of her. She still clutched his wrists trapped between them, and he rolled over, her clinging on. He moved up on his knees, then stood, and she still hung on, wrapping her legs around his waist.

He jolted to shake her off. "You fucking bitch."

They flopped backwards onto the sofa, and the shock of it was a thief, nabbing her breath and stealing it away. He was heavy, pressing his shoulder blades over her face. She attempted to move it to the side so she could breathe, but he added force, pinning her head to the sofa.

"Die," he said, shoving his shoulders into her even more.

She wrenched her neck with the swiftness of the movement, but it meant her nose and mouth were free. Sucking in air, she dragged up her remaining strength and lifted her pelvis to dislodge him. He didn't budge. The shape of someone out in her front garden moved past the window, and it would only be seconds now before someone came in to help. Her hands, damp from sweat, itched from her grip on his wrists. He tugged, but she clamped harder, focusing all her attention on keeping hold of him.

It didn't work. His wrists slipped out of her hands, and he jumped up, grabbing her glass then smashing it on the table. The bowl piece shattered, leaving behind a jagged mountain range of sharp spikes protruding from the stem. He faced her, and she propelled herself to her feet, ready to chop at his hand so he dropped the weapon. He reversed to the doorway one small step at a time, staring at her, seemingly trying to break her with his gaze.

Two officers in black gear filled the doorframe behind him, but Helena didn't make direct eye contact. She didn't want Marshall knowing they were there. She hoped they'd stay where they were so she could get some form of confession out of him.

"What are you going to do, kill me with *that*?" she taunted, gesturing to the glass stem. "Are you going to put nail varnish in my mouth and a flower inside me, then sew *me* up, too?"

He'd registered that she knew it was him—his cheeks and forehead slackened, his mouth flopping open, jaw elastic.

"Shut your fucking mouth," he said, face contorting, anger giving it the impetus to form mean lines and hard planes, turning him into a monster.

A demon.

"What, you don't want to talk about what you did to those women? Blimey, you're such a narcissist, I'd have thought you'd have jumped at the chance to brag."

"You don't talk about them," he said, standing still, his arms bowed, biceps flexing.

Those women hadn't stood a chance against him. He was so big, so strong.

"I can talk about whoever I like, especially those who can no longer speak for themselves. I mean, you sorted that, didn't you, making sure they couldn't tell your secrets."

That was a guess, but she'd hit the mark. He frowned, the cogs turning.

"Yes, Suzie told me all about you," she lied. "The flowers outside their room, the nail varnish, the picnic, the camping in the garden. Did you think leaving the bowl and strawberries was a nice touch? And let's not forget you getting Jacob to steal money so you could buy booze and fags. Why couldn't you just steal it yourself? Too *scared*?"

Fuck, she'd gone too far.

His features tightened. "They deserve to be dead. I should have killed them years ago, the little cows."

That'll do, thanks.

She nodded at the coppers.

Marshall bolted forward, the remains of the glass heading straight for her neck. The officers flashed into the room, grabbed him between them, and cuffed him inside seconds, the glass stem falling to the floor. Helena blew out a breath, her heart going crazy, adrenaline flushing her system, satisfaction at pushing Marshall's buttons giving her a heady rush.

She stepped forward and stared into the eyes of a killer. "Franklin Marston, Marshall Rogers, I'm arresting you on suspicion of murder…" She recited what had to be said, and it seemed he was piercing her psyche with his mad eyes. Unnerved for a couple of seconds, she shook it off, straightening her shoulders. "May you rot in Hell, you filthy piece of shit."

She left the room, going to open the front door, and Andy stood on the other side. The officers carted Marshall past her, and he spat in her face. She left it there until he'd been put inside the meat wagon, then cuffed it off. Turning, she went inside, straight to the bottle of wine, and took a long swig.

Andy stood in the doorway. "I won't say anything if you don't." He gestured to the bottle.

"I'm off duty, mate, so you can stuff that up your arse."

He laughed, and Helena joined in, his low and throaty, hers a tad sharp and high.

Hysteria. It got to the best of people.

CHAPTER TWENTY-FOUR

*U*thway opened the storage container door, and a shaft of light blinded her. It was stronger than before, when his friend had come in, and time had passed, so she could only assume it was a new day. He left it open and strode towards her, anger stripping his face of any speck of kindness he might have lurking inside him. It would be somewhere deep and hidden, she knew that much.

"On your feet," he said. "You're a right shit state and need a wash."

It was a struggle getting up with her wrists tied, but she managed it. Funny how standing in front of him naked didn't matter anymore. He knew her body, the dips and curves, so trying to hide them was pointless.

She glanced down at herself. Grit and dirt from the corner covered her skin, and that didn't matter either. He'd kill her at some point, so a bit of filth wouldn't hurt. Not half as much as what he probably had planned. She'd tracked him for months after bodies had washed up on the shore, ancient symbols carved into their skin. Always the same ones. They'd drafted in an expert, and eventually they'd discovered what the circle with the strange etchings inside it meant: I am God; you will obey.

It was something he'd said to a potential victim, but she'd managed to get away. Emilija, from Lithuania, had helped Helena with information that had led to her finding out where Uthway was holed up.

"Why the symbols?" Helena had asked.

"They did not listen to him, so he killed them. It was his message to the rest of us," Emilija had said. He is God; we must obey. We have to do what he wants with those men. They are getting us ready for sale. We must then obey our new masters."

Helena shivered at the recollection of Emilija speaking as though she still had to feel that way and do those things.

Uthway laughed. "Cold, are you? You'll be a damn sight fucking colder in a minute."

He grabbed her elbow, digging his fingers in, and dragged her to the entrance. Helena blinked in the harsh light, blinded again for a moment, then her vision adjusted. They were near the edge of the cliff, the storage container one of many perched on top of a concrete expanse, some red, some green, some blue. He moved down the two steps and tugged her with him, and she winced at the sharpness of rogue stones digging into her feet. Her container was the last in a row, closest to the ledge. He took her down the side of it, where several black buckets filled with water sat in the shape of a flower, one in the middle, the rest grouped around it.

He untied the ropes, and blessed relief filled her at the same time as a burning set up on her skin, pulsing, itching.

"No point running," he said. "I've got blokes posted everywhere. I'll let you wash yourself." He pointed to a sponge, a cup, some bodywash, and shampoo. "Hurry up. There's people who want to meet you."

Helena thought about Emilija and who those people undoubtedly were. Wasn't Helena too old to be sold in the sex slave trade? "I'm not young enough for them."

"Nah, some of the old duffers like women your age. They've got a bit more experience. I've tried the goods, and I reckon you're good to go." He jabbed a finger at the buckets. "Get a fucking move on."

She dipped her hands and arms into one bucket, the sting of her wrists almost too much from the ice-cold water. It perked her up, bringing life to her weary bones. Sluicing her face had never felt so good, though, and she picked up the cup to pour water over her head. It took her a while to get clean all over, her body aching from the abuse, from her scrunched-up *position in the corner, and even though the sun was out, she shivered from the chill.*

He threw her a navy-blue towel with that weird insignia stitched into it in gold thread, and she wrapped herself in it, using one corner to soak up some of the water in her hair while working out exactly where they were. It was the lowest part of the Smaltern coast. There was no beach, and the sea, near the base, was as deep as it was farther out. To her left, then left again, the cliff sloped downwards, leading to a road which, in turn, led to town.

If she ran that way, someone would catch up with her, or worse, shoot her in the back. But if she moved forward…

She pelted across the grass, letting go of the towel, and leapt off the ledge, staring down at a flat, calm sea waiting to greet her in its fluid arms. She didn't scream, didn't even think, just let herself be in the moment. The slap of her feet on the surface had her gasping, then she was submerged, shooting down at speed into depths unknown, her lungs bursting, a voice whispering in her head that this was it, this was how she was going to die.

She struggled against the momentum then, pushing upwards, using her feet as flippers, her arms seemingly useless, without strength, to shove the water aside and get her to the top. The closer she got to life, the sun appeared as a filtered circle, its rays casting light, illuminating specks of sea filth bobbing along. She breached the surface and gasped for air, treading water, blinking, getting her bearings.

Then she swam towards the direction of town, glancing over her shoulder once to see Uthway at the top of the cliff, staring her way, and she wondered why he didn't get one of his rifles and shoot her.

"I'm coming for you, bitch!" he shouted, the words just about reaching her.

"No," she said to herself, "I'm coming for you."

Helena woke, gasping for breath, her limbs heavy, as if she'd swum in that bloody cold sea all over again. She blinked away the image of her dragging herself onto the shingle and waving down a woman walking her dog. Helena had still been naked, and it hadn't mattered again. Nothing had mattered except ringing Andy to let him know where Uthway was.

She forced herself out of bed and had a shower, pissed off with her nightmares, which would plague her until Uthway had been caught, and probably after that, too.

Clothes on, she headed for Andy's, waiting by the kerb for him to come out. At the station, Louise called Helena over. Helena waved Andy on, and he nodded, going up the stairs.

"What's up?" Helena leant on the front desk.

"Got another body, guv," Louise said. "Well, three, but two are from a road traffic accident yesterday—a Laura Brown and her two-year-old son from Lincoln Road. The other one is—"

"Wait, what?" Had Helena heard that right? "Lincoln Road, you say?"

"Yes."

"Fuck. Okay, how did the accident happen?"

Louise tapped on her keyboard and stared at her monitor. "She was holding her son, running out of an alley behind the Lincoln Road houses. She rushed out into the road, and they got mowed down by a vehicle. SUV. A man was seen at the end of the alley when the car hit them, then he ran the other way. House-to-house enquiries were carried out, but not everyone was home to answer questions. Officers are there again now, trying to catch people before they go to work."

Could Laura have been running from Marshall? Helena had told Laura not to let him in, but what if he broke in and she'd had to run? Guilt swished in her belly. There wasn't anything else she could have done, though. At the time, it hadn't been likely Marshall would even go to Laura's. She hadn't been in imminent danger.

Or so I thought.

"Christ. And the other one?" She swallowed hard.

"Young girl, Elsa Pastle, thirteen. Possible cliff-jumper, but a bunch of red roses washed up on the shore a few metres down from where she did, so it seems a bit suss. Thought it would be something you'd need to know about. She was found yesterday afternoon, and Zach dealt with her, so you might want to give him a ring."

Red roses… Helena's skin prickled with dread. "Okay. Yes. On that now."

She bounded up the stairs then into the incident room.

"Guv?" Olivia called.

"Yes?"

"The reason Franklin/Marshall's NI number went cold is because he was paid cash in hand. His boss admitted to it on the phone just now."

"Righty ho." Helena went into her office. Using the desk phone, she dialled Zach's number at the morgue, and he answered straight away. "Hi," she said. "It's Helena. I hear you have three new bodies—a woman and her son, and a cliff-jumper."

"Good morning to you, too, and yes, it's lovely to hear from you."

"Sorry," she said. "The pleasantries will have to wait. This is urgent."

"I'm only messing. Yes, Laura and William Brown, RTA, and Elsa Pastle, although she didn't jump, she was pushed. Fingertip marks on her back."

"Bloody hell. Forensics have the roses, I take it?"

257

"Yes. Cellophane wrapper, so you might get lucky if whoever held them had greasy fingers and left a print the water didn't manage to wash away."

"We wouldn't *be* that lucky," she said. "Her parents have been dealt with, yes?"

"As far as I'm aware. Why, didn't you do it?"

"Um, no. I was at home, in no state to work. I had to give statements. We pulled Marshall in last night. He's the Walker killer."

"What? Bloody hell! I can't believe it was him!"

"I know. Could have been me—that's what was going through my head, so I didn't think it was wise to go back to work and question him, and I wouldn't be allowed to anyway, what with our connection. That's a job for Andy. A night in a cell might make Marshall more likely to talk."

"I'm really sorry it was him," Zach said, sounding shocked. "Are you okay?"

"Apart from knowing I was in a relationship with a killer? Yes, I'm okay. Let's not talk about this now. I have to go and watch Andy speak to him, and now there are three more people to ask Marshall about."

"You think they're to do with him?"

"Laura Brown was his next-door neighbour, and the roses relating to Elsa…"

"I see. Which reminds me. Suzie Walker. Purple nail varnish in her mouth, plastic forget-me-nots down below." He sighed. "He really is a sicko."

"I know, and I didn't pick up on it at all. Okay, I spotted the temper, the switch from charming to attempting to control, but I'd never have put him down as a killer. Just goes to show, doesn't it, that they walk among us, hiding in plain sight, there, *right there*, and we walk past them, get served by them in shops, whatever, or in Marshall's case, he's in your fucking kitchen or bathroom, putting up tiles. Bloody frightening." Icy fingertips dotted up her spine. "Did you get any feedback on the blood found beside Callie?"

"Fake."

She couldn't understand what that had been in aid of. "Right, I must be getting on. I'll catch up with you later about another date."

"I was going to ask. Yep. Speak soon."

She placed the receiver in the dock and hauled in a breath. Andy had a man to speak to, and she wanted a proper confession.

Helena sat in front of a monitor in a small room and watched the screen.

Marshall seemed to have shrunk overnight, as though his usual bravado that pumped up his muscles had now deserted them. Andy and Phil sat opposite, while one of the duty solicitors sat beside him, a morose-looking man in his fifties, Garth Trent, who always seemed as though he needed a dose of good news to entice his lips up instead of being perpetually downwards.

The interview had gone well so far, with Marshall blaming Franklin for the murders, him stating he had two sides of himself, so it wasn't his fault. Helena didn't believe he needed a medical evaluation just yet, so through Andy's earpiece, she told him to press on.

"We found Callie Walker's fingernails in your house last night," Andy said. "Got anything to say about that?"

Marshall shrugged.

"What about the blood on Callie's carpet?"

"Franklin says it was to remind him of the foster mother. The blood at her house after…"

What?

"As well as Suzie Walker, three people were found dead yesterday." Andy stared at him. "Do you know anything about that?"

"I don't, but Franklin might."

Phil coughed.

"What do you think Franklin might know about your next-door neighbour, Laura Brown, and her little boy, William?" Andy asked.

Marshall shrugged yet again. "The silly cow ran, didn't she."

Helena wanted to slap him.

Andy went on, "And what about Elsa Pastle? Do *you* know anything about her?"

"She's just some kid. Had to get rid of her. She might have talked."

"Am I speaking to *you* right now?"

"Who the hell else are you speaking to? Fuck me…"

"What's your name?"

"Marshall, you know it is."

"Only, you said you didn't know anything about it but Franklin might, yet you just spoke to me as Marshall, telling me about Laura, William, and Elsa. What am I supposed to make of that?" Andy drummed his fingertips on the desk.

Helena was glad she'd followed her gut and hadn't sent Marshall off to be assessed. He was pulling a fast one, the bastard.

"Piss off." Marshall folded his arms across his chest and slumped in the chair, dipping his chin to his chest.

Andy said, "Pending our investigations, and in light of what you just said, we will be adding the charge of suspected murder of Laura Brown, William Brown, and Elsa Pastle to the list along with Suzie Walker, Emma Walker, and Callie Walker."

"There's more," Marshall said.

A jolt of surprise had Helena sitting straighter.

"Will you be telling us who *else* you've killed?" Andy asked.

"Some girls, an old bitch who fostered me, and Mr Jeffs, the wanker."

What about Mr and Mrs Walker?

Anger burned through Helena, and she rose, staring down at the screen.

"Interview suspended at nine forty-seven." Andy sighed, nodded to the constable in the corner, then left the room, Phil trailing after him.

Helena had work to do, as did her team, poking into who the foster mother might have been and checking the death of Mr Jeffs again. It seemed he hadn't jumped off a cliff after all.

She walked out of the room and into the reception area. Louise called her over.

"Call me nosy," Louise said, "but I've had a look at past reports of teenage girls committing suicide off the cliffs. There are a few of them over the years, and each parent swears the kids wouldn't have done such a thing. Now, I know that's a common thing to say, but what if they're right?"

Helena nodded. "Elsa was pushed, so I get where you're coming from. Sort a list of these girls for me and email it to Olivia. I have to nip to see Jacob Walker and Robbie Naul in a sec to tell them they can go home, but I need to pop upstairs to let Olivia and Phil know they have a busy day of trawling ahead."

"Okay, guv."

Helena went upstairs, putting off going to see Yarworth to give him the pointless breakdown of the case's progression. He never gave a shit, but she felt better for doing it, regardless.

In the incident room, she briefed Olivia and Phil on what she'd discovered. "Ol, Louise is going to email you a list of girls who've jumped off the cliff over the years. I need you to do a bit of poking around to see if they knew Franklin Marston, or his name now, Marshall Rogers. Phil, can you look into Mr Jeffs' death, please, and ring Mrs Featherstone at social services to see if she can possibly give you a list of people who fostered Marshall. If she can't, don't worry, I'll apply for a warrant. I'm also interested to know what you found out about the brakes on Mr Walker's car. Anything?"

"Nothing we can use," Phil said.

Helena sighed. Marshall was probably going to get off that murder charge, as well as Mrs Walker's death, as her doctor and the hospital were standing firm that it had been a heart attack. Maybe they'd never know whether Marshall had killed them. Maybe it had been a lucky coincidence, and Marshall had used their deaths to scare Jacob, Suzie, Callie, and Emma into doing what he wanted.

"Okay, I'm off with Andy to see Jacob and Robbie, so catch you later."

She met Andy at the front desk, and they got in the car. As they drove to the safe house flats, Helena thought about the many people Marshall had murdered. Why had he done it? When she got back to the station later, she'd delve into his past, try to piece together why it had all gone so wrong for him — and why he felt murder was his only option.

And also why he felt he had to be the man in the house.

Thank you so much for reading *The Man in the House*. We truly appreciate it and hope you enjoyed!

Printed in Great Britain
by Amazon